The Tempest

Rebel Hearts, Volume 3

Lily Baldwin

Published by Lily Baldwin, 2022.

THE TEMPEST

First edition. August 9, 2022.

Written by Lily Baldwin.

For Autumn ~ you are my courageous, amazing girl. You inspire me to reach ever higher. I love you so much!

Chapter One

Tempest bent low over her saddle and drove her heels into Storm's flanks. The spirited, chestnut mare surged forward as eager to gallop as her mistress. Wind whipped through Tempest's unbound black curls and a smile spread across her face as the joy of the ride filled her soul-deep.

"Faster, Storm," she cried.

Storm whinnied in reply and charged ahead, her hooves thundering across thick beds of heather, which blanketed the rolling moorland. Overhead, a golden eagle soared, its wings spread wide. Closing her eyes, Tempest dropped the reins. She arched her back and spread her arms out to the side, letting her head fall back.

"I'm flying," she exclaimed, but then her breath hitched as Storm reared up on her hind legs, tossing Tempest to the ground. She landed with a hard thud, forcing the breath from her lungs. Her chest ached. She couldn't move.

"Tempest!"

A masculine voice called her name, the timber deep and familiar. An instant later, clear blue eyes, framed by furrowed black brows, hovered over her. "Tempest, speak to me!"

She gasped, at last pulling air into her lungs. "Caleb!"

Relief shaped his features as he pressed a kiss to her forehead, his lips firm and sensual. "Praise be to all the Saints. When I saw ye fall, I...I thought I lost ye. How could I ever go on without ye?"

With a shaky hand, she reached up and cupped his cheek. "Ye needn't fear. We'll always be together, now and forever."

A smile broke across his face. "Ye make me a happy man." He gathered her close and stood, cradling her tenderly in his arms. "I love ye, Tempest."

She wrapped her arms around his neck. "And I love ye."

"Then marry me," Caleb blurted, his blue gaze filled with hope. "Marry me and make me the luckiest man in the Highlands!"

"Aye," she exclaimed. "I will marry ye!"

He closed his eyes and lowered his lips a breath from hers. "Tempest," he whispered.

"Aye," she replied, breathlessly.

"Ye're..." he began, but then his words trailed off.

"Aye," she urged him.

His eyes flew open, but the warmth she had glimpsed in their blue depths was gone. His expression hardened. Cold dread entered her soul. His gaze narrowed on her. "Ye're the last woman I would ever choose to marry," he snarled.

Tempest jerked awake. Her heart pounded. Her dream had felt so real. She could still feel the warmth of Caleb's embrace and the security of his gentle concern, but with a screech of frustration, she shoved her blanket down and swung her legs over the side of the bed.

Her dream had become a nightmare.

A nightmare that too closely mirrored reality.

She had no idea what she had done to earn Caleb's disdain, but his coolness toward her had been growing over the past weeks. And no matter how she tried, she couldn't get him alone long enough to confront him over the matter.

Resting her head in her hands, she remembered how different Caleb had been toward her when he'd first come to Castle Bron.

On the day they met, Tempest had been rushing around the keep, making certain that Castle Bron was ready for her sister's return. Upon Lady Elora's arrival, she introduced two new companions, Nathan Campbell, whom her sister eventually married, and Nathan's closest friend, Caleb.

Caleb was a bounty hunter with a quiet yet compelling presence who never lost control and had a preference for solitude. His tall, well-muscled physique moved with an easy grace, and his striking blue eyes were deeply set beneath a strong, serious brow.

When they had first locked eyes, her breath caught, and her stomach danced.

Even now, perched on the edge of her bed, a smile upturned her lips as she remembered his well-mannered greeting, after which, to her surprise, he had asked to bed down in the stables for the duration of his stay, politely refusing a chamber within the keep. It was Tempest who had shown him the way to the stables. As they walked together, she remembered finding herself uncharacteristically tongue-tied...

"Welcome to Castle Bron," she managed to say.

He dipped his head slightly to her. "Thank ye."

Seldom quiet, she searched her mind for something to say to the sexy newcomer, but she suddenly felt so uncertain. When they arrived at the stables, she showed him to the ladder that led up to the loft, and he smiled down at her. "Thank ye," he said again.

Her cheeks burned. She wanted to reply, but her tongue felt thick in her mouth. She stood in place, staring up at him, unspeaking; until, at last, she finally blurted, "I love to ride!"

An amused look passed over his features. He smiled slightly, his eyes warm as he continued to meet her gaze, but he did not reply.

"I...I come to the stables often." She swallowed hard.

Still, he did not speak.

Feeling like a fool, she longed to run away, but her legs refused to cooperate. Finally, her heart racing, her legs trembling, she managed a step back and then another. Just as she was about to turn on her heel and sprint away from the intoxicating stranger, the corners of his mouth upturned in a slight smile and he said, "I'm glad."

A smile broke across her face, and her heart leapt. Not knowing what else to do or say, she waved and backed away only to trip on an overturned bucket.

He rushed to her aid. "Are ye hurt?"

"Nay, I—" she started to explain that she was constantly tripping over her skirts while in the stables, but her breath caught when his strong hand clasped her waist. Heart pounding, mouth dry, she lost herself in the warmth of his gaze. They stood a breath apart for several moments, eyes locked. She felt as if something within him reached across the space between them and caressed her very soul. Unable to withstand the powerful feelings rushing through her, she tore her gaze away and sprinted from the stables.

Over those initial weeks, she had spent little time in his company as he often kept to himself. Still, when she did see him, he had always been kind to her, and despite his reserved nature, Tempest had felt his presence profoundly. He carried himself with a quiet confidence that stole her breath and made her palms sweat.

Alone in her chamber, she closed her eyes, her mind revisiting the time Caleb had danced with her in the great hall. In fairness, he had only done so at Nathan's urging. Still, while they had danced, his lips upturned slightly, again hinting at a rarely seen smile. And as the music slowed, their eyes had met. In his gaze, she had glimpsed the same hunger that made her own heart long for his touch.

Or at least she thought she had...

She knew those fleeting moments may have been nothing more than the fancies of her own imagination.

A mirthless laugh fled her lips as she stood and crossed to the casement. Her heart brimming with doubt, she threw open the shutters. Scanning the courtyard below, her gaze settled on the stables. She wondered whether Caleb was still asleep in the hay loft, the sound of his restful breaths mingling with the gentle whinnies and snorts of the clan's horses. She imagined him lying on his pallet, his eyes closed, his dark lashes fanning out across his cheeks, and a peaceful set to his square jaw.

"Stop it," she snapped at herself.

It was a small wonder she could still conjure his ruggedly handsome features so easily as it had been weeks since she had spoken to him for more than a fleeting moment. When her sister and Nathan had still been at Castle Bron, Caleb would come to the castle for the evening meal; however, the laird and lady of the keep had traveled north to visit Nathan's family. Now, Caleb never set foot in the great hall.

Expelling a long sigh, Tempest watched the sun break over the distant horizon. A new day had begun. Squaring her shoulders, she closed her eyes against the ache in her heart just as a soft rapping sounded at the door.

"Enter," she called.

Her maid, Firtha, hastened inside with a tunic draped over her arm. "Good morrow, Lady Temperance," she said quickly, her brow pinched with worry.

Firtha was tall and skinny with angular, bony shoulders and a long neck. The skin over her pinched face was pulled taut and held a pale hue without a hint of rosiness across her cheeks. As always, she looked as if she were about to burst into tears.

"I've mended yer skirt, my lady," she said, shaking her head disapprovingly. "I do wish ye'd be more careful. Ye might have broken yer neck."

Tempest raised a brow at her fretful maid. "My foot caught on the gate, and I scraped my knee."

"Ye shouldn't have been in the stall with yer unruly mare in the first place. Arthur and Jacob tend the horses. Ye're a lady. In fact, with yer sister gone, ye are the lady of Castle Bron."

Accustomed to ignoring her maid's relentless scolding, Tempest stretched her arms over her head. "I will dress as there is much to do today."

Firtha hastened to the wardrobe and hung the freshly mended tunic on a peg before withdrawing a dark green tunic and cream colored surcote.

"Just the tunic, please," Tempest said, taking another deep breath against her rising frustration.

Firtha turned and met her gaze. "But Lady Temperance, 'tis most improper—"

"We have the same conversation every morning," Tempest interrupted. "I have no intention of wearing a surcote today, just like yesterday and the day before that. I could go on."

Firtha pressed her lips in a grim line as if choking back a string of reprimands before finally muttering, "Aye, my lady." Frowning, the maid returned the surcote to the wardrobe, then crossed to Tempest's side.

After helping Tempest don the soft woolen tunic, Firtha cinched a leather belt tightly around Tempest's waist. And, just as she did every morning, Tempest loosened the knot until the belt sat low on her hips. Firtha shook her head with disapproval but held her tongue, for which Tempest was grateful. Running her fingers through her thick, black curls, she turned and faced her maid. "Agnes is expecting me in the kitchen."

"Very well, Lady Temperance," Firtha replied, her voice heavy with resignation. Casting Tempest a fleeting look of displeasure, she started to straighten the bed linens.

"Fritha, will ye never call me Tempest? Even Elora has ceased calling me Temperance."

Fritha released the blanket she held and put her hands on her hips. "Forgive my defiance, my lady, but ye were first given the pet name when ye were a wee child because of yer impulsive nature. I believe it only encourages yer recklessness. Yer given name is perfectly respectable, and it means restraint, which is the very thing yer sister asked me to teach ye when she made me yer maid on yer tenth birthday."

Tempest knew that Firtha was right, at least about Elora's reasoning for making Firtha her maid. Elora had hoped that Firtha might be a positive influence on Tempest, but regardless of her maid's tireless efforts at schooling Tempest in decorum and the gentle role of a clan's lady, Tempest continued to follow her own heart and mind, which meant Firtha was upset most of the time.

With her hair unbound and her tunic flowing freely, Tempest left her chamber and her anxious maid behind and made her way to the kitchen where Agnes awaited her.

"Good morrow, my lady."

Trying to put her dream, Caleb, and Firtha's nagging out of her mind, Tempest took a deep breath and smiled. "Good morrow, Agnes."

Agnes had always reminded Tempest of an oak tree in Autumn. She was tall, solidly built with a ruddy complexion, and bright red hair. With her great height, she stood out among the undercooks who were already hastening about the kitchen, salting meat and baking bread. In the midst of the bustle, Agnes and Tempest planned the day's menu. They decided on leftover meat pies and smoked herring for the noon meal, and pheasant dumplings, peas, and leek and mutton stew for the evening meal.

"What shall we have for dessert?" Agnes asked but gave Tempest a knowing smile.

"Stewed apples, of course."

Agnes smiled. "I awoke this morrow somehow knowing ye would make that very request. Ye'll be happy to know that we already have several bushels peeled and ready to be boiled down."

Tempest threw her arms around Agnes's neck. "Ye're the dearest and the best."

Agnes laughed and squeezed her tightly. "And ye're a blessing and a joy, my lady."

Tempest's smile faltered. "I'm glad ye think so. Now, if ye can only convince Firtha of that."

Agnes waved her hand dismissively. "Ye keep speaking yer mind. I've admired yer spirit since ye were a wee lass. Sure, ye're quick to lose yer temper, but ye're just as quick to laugh. Anyway, Clan Brodie thrives because of its strong and courageous ladies, and Firtha would do well to remember that."

"She means well," Tempest said quickly. "And, in fairness, she is trying to do what she feels is best for me."

Agnes smiled and cupped Tempest's cheek lovingly. "The only thing that could rival the size of yer temper is yer heart, my lady. And I love ye for it—we all do."

Tempest's heart swelled. Tears stung her eyes. "Thank ye, Agnes. I needed to hear those words."

"Och, pet," Agnes crooned, pulling Tempest close once more. "Ye're missing Lady Elora, aren't ye?"

"Aye," Tempest said, which wasn't untrue. She did miss her sister, but that wasn't the cause of her dampened spirits nor was Firtha's nagging. It was her dream and Caleb's cool regard, but she dared not confess to Agnes the true reason for her distress. In fact, she hadn't confided the depth of her feelings for Caleb to anyone. She gently pulled herself free from Agnes's embrace and took a deep breath. "But ye needn't fash yerself. Elora and Nathan will be home soon enough, and I will do my best to ensure that Castle Bron runs smoothly while they are away. With that in mind, I will let ye get to work and I'll see how things are progressing in the pantry."

Happy for a fresh distraction, Tempest entered the pantry where Alison, Castle Bron's pantler, sat on a stool, cradling her newborn bairn in her arms. Alison's blond curls were pulled back in a simple plait, and her green eyes shone brightly as she smiled when Tempest entered the cramped space.

"Good morrow," Tempest said briskly, determined to think of anything other than Caleb. Wanting to immerse herself in her work, she skipped over the usual niceties she exchanged with her friend and took up her quill and the ledger. "What is the loaf count from yesterday?"

Alison raised her brow at Tempest. "Ye're rather eager this morning."

"I am," Tempest replied simply.

Alison gave her an assessing look. "Ye don't quite seem like yerself."

Tempest chose the same excuse for her mood that had appeased Agnes. After all, it wasn't truly a lie. "I'm missing Elora."

"Of course ye are. We all are," Alison said, her voice soothing. "Actually, I'm surprised ye didn't go with them."

"Why?" Tempest asked, looking up from the ledger.

Alison lifted her shoulders. "Ye seemed to get on well with Nathan's sister, Cait. I would have thought ye'd jumped at the chance to see her again."

Alison was right. Under normal circumstances, Tempest never would have missed the opportunity to visit Clan Campbell, but ever since Caleb had come to Castle Bron, nothing had felt normal. She forced a smile to her face. "I long to see Cait again. She is such a nervous creature but also honest and kind. Still, I wanted this opportunity to prove myself to Elora."

"Is that really why ye stayed?" Alison asked softly.

Tempest cast Alison a wary look. "Why would ye think otherwise?"

The pantler shrugged her shoulders. "'Tis just that ye ken yer sister loves ye."

Tempest set her quill down and looked Alison square in the eye. "Clearly, ye have yer own idea about why I stayed behind. So, out with it already."

Alison lifted her shoulders. "Well, I have wondered whether a certain Highlander influenced yer decision."

Tempest's cheeks suddenly burned. "How...how did ye know?"

"I have eyes don't I," Alison said with a coy smile. "But when ye stayed behind that's when I knew for certain."

Tempest leaned back against the basket of bread loaves on the shelf behind her and breathed out a sigh of relief.

Alison chuckled. "Secrets are heavy things, aren't they?"

Tempest nodded. "How long have ye known?"

A glimmer of excitement shone in Alison's eyes. "I thought I saw a spark between ye and Cait's brother, Peter, when he first arrived at Castle Bron. But when ye stayed behind, I knew it was because ye were too nervous to see him again."

Tempest's smile faltered. "Cait's brother? But he's not..." Her words trailed off.

Alison's brows raised before she bent over and laid her sleeping bairn in the basinet at her feet. Then she whirled back around to face Tempest. "Who is he?"

Tempest clapped her hands over her face. "Do not ask me that?" she mumbled beseechingly.

"'Tis too late now, my lady. Ye must tell me."

Keeping her face hidden, Tempest refused to speak.

"Let me see," Alison said pensively.

Tempest dropped her hands and held her breath while she watched Alison pace the slim corridor of the pantry.

"It couldn't be Cait's oldest brother, Matthew. He's too old." Alison muttered as if to herself. "Ye've never shown any of our warriors special favor." Then suddenly, she gasped and whirled around to face Tempest. "Nay, he cannot be the one!"

Tempest swallowed hard. "What if he is?"

"But my lady," Alison admonished. "Caleb is a bounty hunter and a commoner!"

Tempest's nostrils flared. "Why should that matter? He's a fine man...I...I think, anyway."

Alison dropped to her knees in front of Tempest and took hold of her hands. "Caleb *is* a fine man, of that I've no doubt, and would make another lass a wonderful husband, but—"

"What other lass?" Tempest demanded, jerking her hands away.

Alison stood up and pressed her hands to her brow. "Och, yer jealous about the possibility of another lass ...'tis worse than I thought."

Tempest set her hands on her hips. "Nathan was a bounty hunter, and Elora married him."

Alison raised a brow at her. "Nathan is also the son of a laird."

Tempest's arms dropped to her side. She had never given any thought to Caleb's station. To her, he had always been the same as Nathan, but Alison was right. Nathan was the son of a laird. Caleb was the nameless son of no one.

Her stomach twisted. "Oh, God."

"How far have things progressed between ye both? I mean ye haven't...given yerself to him?"

"Of course not!"

Alison expelled a slow breath of relief as she sat down on her stool. "This conversation will stay between us. No one must ever know—"

"Elora knows that I care for him, or at least she might. I've never spoken of my true feelings—"

"What are yer true feelings?"

Tempest plopped back down on her seat and cradled her head in her hands. "I do not ken."

"Has he made his feelings known to ye?"

Fury once more coursed through Tempest's veins. She looked up and met the pantler's gaze. "I've tried to speak to him," she snapped. Then she blew out a long breath, fighting for calm. "Forgive me, Alison. I'm just frustrated. The truth is that I've tried to speak with Caleb, but either he is nowhere to be found or, when I have been able to track him down, he barely speaks to me. Then, predictably, I lose my temper, and nothing is truly said."

Alison nodded. "I have noticed that he stopped coming to the great hall for dinner."

"He doesn't want to see me." Tempest stood and clenched her fists. "And what truly infuriates me is that..." Her voice dropped. Tears stung her eyes. "I long to see him."

Alison shook her head with vehemence. "Ye must forget him!"

Tempest's nostrils flared. She never liked being told what to do, even by a trusted confidant like Alison. Standing, Tempest forced a smile to her lips. "I will," she lied. "And ye must forget as well." She gave a careless wave of her hand. "I'm ten and seven now, a woman grown, but I've no interest in marriage, whether to Caleb or anyone else. When Elora feels the time is right, she'll arrange a suitable match for me."

Judging by the look of relief that washed over Alison's face, Tempest knew that her placating words had gleaned the desired effect.

"I'm glad to hear that, my lady. None of our kin faults ye for wearing yer simple tunics or riding yer fearsome horse astride, excepting Firtha, of course. But some conventions must be upheld."

Forcing a smile to her lips, Tempest set her quill and ledger on the shelf. "We can finish the inventory on the morrow. I need some fresh air. I think I will take Storm for a ride."

"Excellent, my lady," Alison said, spurring her on. "Race across the riding fields. Ye'll feel all the better for it."

Tempest turned on her heel and marched from the pantry. She knew what she had to do to feel better, and for once, riding Storm was not the answer. She had to confront Caleb, and this time, she was determined to say her piece.

"Where are ye off to, my lady?" Agnes called to her as she crossed through the kitchen.

"I'm going to speak my mind!"

"Saints preserve us," Agnes exclaimed.

Tempest narrowed her eyes as she pushed the kitchen door wide and stormed through the great hall toward the courtyard. "The only one who needs protection from the saints is Caleb," she muttered to herself.

Just then clear blue eyes came to the fore of her thoughts, causing her chest to tighten. As she stepped into the stables, her heart pounded in her ears. Her palms started to sweat just at the possibility of speaking to him. She swallowed her screech of frustration. No one had ever been able to unnerve her like him. With long strides, she approached the loft where he slept and set her hands on her hips.

"Caleb, I must speak with ye," she called up to him.

But only silence followed.

"Caleb," she shouted, her face upturned. "Do not ignore me!"

Still, he did not reply.

She crossed to the ladder. "I'm coming up. Ye've no choice but to hear what I have to say."

Grabbing the hem of her tunic, she tucked it into her belt, and took a deep breath.

It was now or never.

She quickly ascended. When her gaze crested beyond the loft floor, all she could see was his neatly rolled pallet.

"Blast," she cursed. He had already arisen and left the stables for the day. Scurrying back down the ladder, she noticed then that his horse was gone. "Blast!"

She paced the area in front of the stalls. How she wished she could set a trap for him. In her mind's eye, she saw him dangling upside down by a rope tied around his ankle, completely and utterly at her mercy. He would have no choice but to listen to her every word. She seized a rope, ready to set her plan in motion but froze as a new image came to mind—one of her accidentally trapping the stablemaster instead.

She cursed again, furious at her own desperation. A wave of emotion shot through her. Crossing to Storm's stall, she flung open the gate. After quickly fastening her mare's bridle, she climbed the side enclosure, inserting her slippered feet between the wood slats like a ladder, and seized a fistful of Storm's black mane. Then she hitched up her tunic and swung her leg over her mare's bare back. Sitting astride, her fists clutching Storm's mane, she drove her heels into the mare's chestnut rump and tore out of the stall, leaving a cloud of dust in her wake.

She thundered through the front gate, galloped over the riding fields, and set out across the open moors. The thrill of the ride shot through her. A smile that her fury could never suppress broke across her face. She was doing what she was made for. She would ride until she forgot all about clear blue eyes and broad shoulders. But as she raced over the heather, she knew she could sooner graze her fingertips across the summer sky than forget about the compelling commoner who had captured her heart.

Chapter Two

Caleb steered the unwieldy plough through the earth, straining to keep the oxen in check while Declan, the captain of the Brodie warriors, encouraged the beasts with a light switch. Caleb was not of Clan Brodie, or any other clan for that matter, but he was happy to serve the clan who had given him such a courteous welcome. More than that, the toil gave his mind reprieve from the shadows of his past that always threatened to darken his thoughts.

When the final row of earth was turned, he released the plough and wiped the sweat from his brow.

Declan offered him a costrel. "The sun is hot today."

Caleb nodded, accepting the drink. He took a long draught before handing the vessel back to the older man.

"I'll be making the rounds later this week, if ye'd like to join." Declan asked. His smile crinkled his kind eyes. "Fergus's daughters are still hoping to meet ye."

Caleb shook his head. "Save yer match making for another man."

"I only meant to make introductions. All three are winsome lasses. One may catch yer fancy."

Caleb raised his brow at the captain. "I've no doubt they are all good and obliging lasses, but I've no intention of wooing a Brodie lass when I only mean to leave yer territory upon Nathan's return."

Brows drawn, Declan asked, "What is so important out there? By yer own admission, ye have no family."

Caleb shrugged his shoulders. "I have my own plans."

"Aye, to be alone." Declan said grimly. "Consider a brighter future for yerself. Ye can build a life here. Have a family."

Caleb shook his head. "Marriage, family...that is for some men but not for me." He started to turn away.

"What about Lady Tempest?" Declan said in a quiet voice for Caleb's ears alone.

Caleb whirled around, locking eyes with the older man. "What about her?"

Declan rubbed the back of his neck. "Well, I noticed that the two of ye—"

Caleb closed the distance between them. "She is a lady," he said in a low voice. He did not speak sharply, but his tone held a warning. "Good morrow, Declan."

"Good morrow," the captain replied.

With a dip of his head, Caleb turned on his heel and marched away toward where his mount was grazing. Straightaway, Lady Tempest came to the fore of his thoughts. In his mind's eye he saw her unbound black curls and intense blue eyes.

"Nay," he said out loud to himself. He reached his horse and pressed his forehead to the black stallion's muzzle. Then he swung up in the saddle and nudged his heels into his horse's flanks. He needed to rid his thoughts of her. He had no business dwelling on one of Clan Brodie's ladies, especially one who had only just turned ten and seven while he was nearly eight years her senior. But age was not the only thing that separated them.

She was vibrant and full of life while he was a miserable bastard.

She was a lady, and he was nothing—he didn't even have a name to give her.

Wishing to escape his thoughts, he urged his horse into a gallop. He shouldn't even be at Castle Bron. He had intended to leave after Nathan and Elora had finally married, but then the newlyweds had decided to travel north. This, alone, would not have been enough to keep Caleb at Castle Bron, but Nathan had asked Caleb to stay on to protect Lady Tempest who had drawn the interest of their ruthless neighbor Egan, laird of Clan MacKintosh. But Tempest had not always been what Egan coveted most.

Elora and Tempest's father had been a cruel man in life. In fact, it was believed that their mother's ill-health stemmed from having to endure his continuous abuse. She passed away when the sisters were very young. But losing his wife hadn't softened the laird of Clan Brodie. When Elora reached the age to marry, he promised her to Laird MacKintosh. Elora had been horrified, but her father died before he could sign the marriage contract.

Determined never to utter the words 'honor and obey' to such an unkind man as Egan, Lady Elora had concocted a wild plan and went in search of a man reckless enough to set that plan in motion. That was how Elora first met Nathan and Caleb.

In the end, Elora escaped marriage to Egan. However, their ruthless neighbor was still determined to marry a Brodie lady, and having lost his claim to the eldest sister, he set his sights on marrying Tempest.

Now, having given Nathan his word, Caleb was bound to Clan Brodie and its unwed lady, at least until Nathan's return.

A sudden drop of rain on his forehead forced him to look skyward. Storm clouds had gathered overhead, dark and writhing. It bothered him that he had been so preoccupied with thoughts of Tempest that another tempest had moved in without him even noticing. The Heavens opened and unleashed sheets of rain. Then a flash of lightning slashed the sky, followed by a rumble of thunder.

He reined in his mount. Movement to his left caught his eye. In the distance, he saw two children racing across the moors. Turning his horse about, he galloped toward them. As he drew closer, he could see that one of the children was a young lad with nine or ten years. He wore no tunic, and the top of his drenched plaid dragged on the ground while he hastened through the storm, leading a wee lass by the hand. She could not have been seven. Her face crumpled with tears. He reined in his horse a short distance away from them and slid down from his saddle. As he hurried toward them, the lad clenched his fists and stepped in front of the younger child like a shield.

"'Tis all right," Caleb said, squatting down to their height. "I'm a friend."

The lad eyed him. "I've seen ye about with Declan. Ye're kin to our laird."

"Aye," Caleb answered. "In a manner of speaking." He smiled to ease the lad's fear. "Do ye live in the village?"

The lad nodded. Then a roar of thunder blasted their ears and the wee lass sobbed harder. "I'll take ye home," Caleb said. Before the lad could answer, he scooped both children into his arms and set them on his horse's back. Then he swung up behind them. He unwrapped the top of his plaid and encircled the children in the sodden folds before he set off back toward the village. As they drew close, the lad pointed at a woman with a careworn face and a wet shawl draped over her head. She was speaking to Declan.

"'Tis our mum," the lad shouted over the din of the rain.

"Mum!" the wee lass cried.

As they approached, Declan turned and met Caleb's gaze. The strain on his face eased straightaway. Caleb pulled his horse to a halt beside them.

"Collin," the woman cried as a smile broke across her face. "Isla!"

Caleb slid down and lifted the lass off his horse, placing the child straight into her mother's waiting arms. Caleb then turned and reached for the lad, but he shook his head and slid to the ground by himself. His mother pulled him close. Caleb stepped back as the family clung to each other.

Smiling, Declan slapped Caleb on the back. "Ye came through again for our clan," he said. "Anna found me shortly after it began to rain and said that they had gone to forage for herbs earlier but had yet to return. I was just about to gather a band of men to look for them."

"Thank ye," the woman said, Isla still clinging to her neck.

Caleb smiled slightly and dipped his head to the woman who then hastened away to escape the downpour.

"I'll see ye on the morrow," Caleb said to Declan before he turned to mount his horse.

"Will ye not come to the keep for supper?"

Caleb had not entered the keep since Nathan and Lady Elora had left, nor did he intend to. The less he saw Lady Tempest, the better. Soon, the laird and lady of Castle Bron would return, and he could leave Clan Brodie and her black-haired lady behind.

"I'll see ye on the morrow," Caleb repeated. Then he swung up into his saddle and urged his horse toward the castle grounds.

Once inside the stables, Caleb was greeted by Arthur, the stablemaster.

"I'm glad ye've returned. 'Tis a frightful storm," Arthur said as he took Caleb's reins.

"Indeed," Caleb answered.

Arthur was strong and stout with a ring of straggly gray hair around his otherwise bald head. He was a good man whose company Caleb could often find tolerable, but he was a loquacious sort. And, at that moment, Caleb did not feel like making conversation.

Jacob drew Caleb's gaze as the lad exited one of the stalls. He was a lad of ten and two years with thick brown hair, which he wore in a long plait down his back. Like Caleb, Jacob was a man of few words.

"I'll wipe yer stallion down," Jacob offered, but Caleb shook his head. He welcomed the distraction of tending his mount. He led his horse past several stalls, but then he froze, stopping in front of one that was empty. He whirled around, meeting Arthur's gaze. "Where's Storm?"

Arthur shifted his gaze to the empty stall. His eyes shot wide. "Lady Tempest must have taken her out when we were working in the fields."

Caleb's nostrils flared as he turned toward the stable doors, pulling his mount behind him. "Blast her recklessness! When will she learn restraint?" He swung up in the saddle and charged back out into the courtyard. Lightning slashed the bleak sky. Thunder blasted his ears as he set out amidst a tempest to search for the true Tempest, the passionate and impulsive lady of Castle Bron.

Chapter Three

Tempest kept her head low while she gripped Storm with her thighs and raced across the moors. Thunder shook the earth. Lightning raked its bright fingers across the sky, but she was not afraid—she was exhilarated. Wet curls clung to her cheeks. Her tunic was soaked through. The dark clouds above writhed with power, mirroring the passion in her heart that ached to be unleashed. Ahead of her, loomed Castle Bron. Its turreted towers and soaring battlements filled Tempest with pride.

Smiling, she lifted her face to the sky, letting the rain pelt her skin.

"What are ye doing out here?" a voice shouted.

She jerked her head around and spied Caleb riding toward her.

His eyes flashed with anger. "What are ye doing out here?" he demanded again.

She rolled her eyes. "Riding," she called out over the din of the storm.

Leaning forward, he seized her reins and jerked them from her grip.

She gasped. Then her eyes narrowed on him. "How dare ye!"

His nostrils flared but he did not reply. He turned his horse about and drove his heels into his horse's flanks as he shot forward with Storm in tow.

"Caleb, ye go too far!"

Mirroring her mistress's indignation, Storm snorted and pulled at the reins in Caleb's grip, but to no avail. Both lady and mare had no choice but to follow Caleb and his stallion. As they galloped toward Castle Bron, Tempest's heart began to pound harder, but not from the thrill of the ride or from Caleb's proximity or the sight of his broad shoulders, to which his shirt and plaid clung, revealing his powerful muscles. Fury coursed through her, setting her pulse to race.

They rode through the front gate and straight into the stables.

"How dare ye!" Tempest snapped as she slid to the ground.

Caleb's eyes flashed with fury, but when he spoke his voice was calm and controlled. "My lady, I've been scouring the moors for ye for well-nigh an hour now. I was on my way back to the castle to see if ye'd returned when I spotted ye from across the field. And judging by yer uncharacteristically easy pace, 'twas clear to me that ye were in no hurry to reach shelter. Yer recklessness left me with little choice but to take control." He turned away from her, leading his horse into a stall.

"Do not walk away from me!"

"This matter is finished," he said in the same controlled voice, which made her own temper rise to greater heights.

"In my own defense," she began sharply, "the sky was clear when I left. I never meant to be caught in the storm, but since it could not be helped, there's no wrongdoing in enjoying the ride!"

He raised a brow at her but said nothing as he once more turned his back to her.

Her hands clenched in tight fists. "Anyway, what do ye care?"

Caleb stopped walking and turned back around. His inscrutable gaze met hers. "Ye should go to the keep. No doubt

Firtha is beside herself with worry. And if I know Declan, he is likely gathering a band of guards to search for ye as we speak."

Her nostrils flared. "Ye've no right to criticize me!"

"I wasn't criticizing. I was giving ye some advice." Dropping his horse's reins, he stepped closer.

She swallowed hard as she tilted her head back to meet his gaze.

His eyes narrowed on her. "To demonstrate the difference, this is criticism—at this very moment, people who care about ye, who ye profess to love, are likely worried sick over yer absence. Does that mean nothing to ye?"

A lump formed in her throat. She dragged a hand through her wet curls. "Of course it does, but..."

He turned his back to her. Entering the stall, he began brushing his stallion's coat as if Tempest was not even there.

Awash in remorse and anger, she cried out, "Caleb, look at me!"

He ceased grooming his horse and slowly turned and met her gaze.

But her chest tightened at the sight of his impassive eyes. Feeling the sting of tears, she backed away, then turned and hastened toward the keep.

Regret and fury battled for domination in her heart. She felt as if her emotions were spilling past the seams of her flesh.

Why had she not raced back to the castle when it first started to rain like a sensible lady might?

But then, once more, her anger took over. Had she been shaking with fear as she rode back to Castle Bron through the storm, then likely Caleb would have comforted her. Mayhap, he would have even swept her into his arms and cradled her back to the keep.

But that wasn't who she was. She would never be the helpless maid afraid of the gale.

When she passed through the doors into the great hall, the scene that Caleb had predicted met her gaze. Fritha stood wringing her hands, her face stricken while she spoke with Declan. "She's out there, Declan. We must do more!"

"Arthur said that Caleb is searching for her. If he does not bring her back within the hour, then I will assemble—"

"I'm here," Tempest called.

"Lady Temperance," Firtha exclaimed and raced toward her, her pointy elbows jutting out awkwardly as she ran. "Och child, what ye do to my heart." Firtha pulled Tempest into a fierce embrace.

"I'm fine. I was out for a ride."

Firtha drew away slightly, meeting Tempest's gaze. "A lady has no business being beyond the boundaries of Castle Bron and the village on her own."

"I was well within Brodie territory," Tempest shot back. Then she looked to Declan for support. "Declan, please remind Firtha, and later Caleb when ye see him, that I have Elora's blessing to ride Storm on my own."

"Indeed, ye do, my lady, but I'm confident yer sister meant for ye to remain in the riding fields, especially while there is still a threat from our neighbor. If ye had crossed paths with Laird MacKintosh, I've no doubt that he would have tried to abduct ye."

Tempest crossed her arms over her chest. "I never left Brodie territory."

"Think ye Egan MacKintosh honors our borders?" Declan said pointedly.

Her arms dropped to her sides. "Blast," she muttered under her breath. "Ye're right," she said simply. And if she were honest with herself, she had known when she was riding that she had ventured too far, but she had felt so compelled by the ride—the sun on her face, the wind in her hair. The freedom and distance away from the keep had soothed her mounting frustration.

She expelled a slow breath and met Declan's gaze. "Forgive me. I wasn't thinking beyond the moment."

Instantly, Firtha's expression softened. She wrapped her arm around Tempest's shoulders. "There, there," the older woman crooned. "Let us get ye dry and warm before ye catch a fever."

Feeling as powerless as a piece of wood adrift on a wave, Tempest allowed Firtha to lead her through the great hall toward the high dais. Her only consolation was that Caleb had not witnessed her admitting that she'd been wrong.

Soon, she was sitting in a high-backed chair near the hearth in her chamber while several kitchen lads poured steaming buckets of water into a large tub. After it was filled, Firtha helped her out of her wet tunic and kirtle before she eased into the hot water.

"Lean forward and I shall wash yer back," Firtha offered, holding a soapy cloth.

But Tempest forced a slight smile to her face. "Thank ye, but nay. I'm just going to soak for a spell. I will put myself to bed. Ye can retire now."

Firtha nodded. "I can see yer fatigue. Ye really must not push yerself so. Such exercise is not suitable for a lady." The maid gently patted Tempest's hand, which was resting on the edge of the tub. But then Firtha's brows drew together while she examined Tempest's hand more closely. "Don't forget to rub the lanolin into yer skin," Firtha shook her head and sighed. "Ye'd never believe ye were a lady judging by yer hands. Yer sister's are unblemished and smooth as silk."

Tempest choked back the biting remark that longed to flee her lips. "Goodnight, Firtha."

Firtha dipped into a low curtsey. "Good night, my lady."

When the chamber door closed, Tempest laid her head back on the edge of the tub. She knew better than to ride so far from the castle grounds. Still, had she not been so frustrated by Caleb's dismissive behavior toward her, and her continued inability to confront him on the matter, then she never would have been so upset in the first place.

With a screech, she pushed against the sides of the tub and stood, stepping on the soft fur pelt next to the tub. Then she seized the length of linen that Firtha had left for her and began to dry herself off. After donning her night gown, which was un-adorned except for a ruffle at the bottom hem, she climbed into bed and tried to put him out of her mind. But after tossing and turning for what felt like hours, she sat up.

Why could she not dismiss him as easily as he had dismissed her?

And then one of the moments they had shared when he first came to Castle Bron that had been burned into memory came to the fore of her mind.

She had been in the stables brushing Storm's coat when...

Caleb drew close behind her—so close that she could smell his masculine scent and feel the heat from his body.

"Ye need to put more force in yer stroke," he said, his voice low and husky.

Her breath caught as his hand covered hers and slowly guided the brush over her mare's back. She swallowed hard, her heart pounding. His hand was so big and strong. She twisted and looked up to meet his gaze and softly gasped when she saw the heat in his eyes. He drew closer still and slowly raised his hand. The back of his fingers nigh grazed her cheek, but then he snaked his hand away.

"What is it?" she asked.

His nostrils flared. He shook his head and took a step back.

"Nay," she said, reaching out to him. "Please don't go."

Without reply, he turned on his heels and left the stables.

Seizing her pillow, she pressed her face into the covered down. That moment had been real. The heat in his eyes had been real. But then what had she done to douse the flames? She would have no peace until she knew the truth.

In that moment, she was struck by a realization.

It was the middle of the night—she knew exactly where Caleb was at that moment. He would no doubt be asleep in the loft above the stables.

With a deep breath, she pushed the covers off and scooted out of bed. After sliding her feet into her slippers, she seized a shawl from her wardrobe, then opened her chamber door. Candlelight flickered down the empty hallway. Closing the door softly behind her, she padded quietly away from her chamber, but instead of using the stairs to the family rooms, she took the servants stairwell down to the kitchen. Easing open the door into Agnes's herb patch, she cut across the holding corral and slid open the gate that led directly into Storm's stall.

"Wheesht," she whispered when her mare whinnied. She pressed her forehead to Storm's muzzle to quiet her before silently making her way to Arthur's worktable where she lit a candle. Holding the flame aloft, she scanned the stables. Her gaze settled on the ladder and then the loft above.

Squaring her shoulders, she crossed to the ladder, but faltered realizing she could not hold the candle and the hem of her nightdress and reach for one of the rungs. Setting the candle holder down, she tied the shawl around her waist. Then she hitched up her gown, tucked the hem in her makeshift belt, picked the candle back up, and began to climb.

When her gaze crested over the edge of the loft, she saw Caleb stretched out on his pallet. The soft glow of candlelight illuminated his handsome features and the strength of his bare chest. Her heart started to pound. Her mouth ran dry. He shifted suddenly, and she nearly lost her balance. Her heart racing harder than ever, she climbed the rest of the way onto the loft floor and stood at the opposite end of where he lay.

Clasping tightly to the candle, she whispered, "Caleb."

But he did not stir.

"Caleb," she hissed louder.

He jerked upright. She sucked in a sharp breath. They locked eyes. An instant later, he seized his shirt, which he quickly pulled over his head. "What are ye doing here?"

Holding fast to her courage, she said, "I need to speak with ye."

He raked his hand through his hair. "Could this not wait until the morrow?"

"I've tried to speak with ye during the daylight hours, but either ye're nowhere to be found or we start to argue before I've managed to say my piece."

He raised a brow at her. "I do not argue. Ye lose yer temper."

Her brow furrowed. "That's not true," she snapped, but then realized her outburst had accomplished nothing other than to prove his point. "Why must ye antagonize me?"

"May I remind ye that 'tis ye who've awoken me from a peaceful slumber." He leaned back against the wall and gave her an assessing look. "Say yer piece then."

She swallowed hard, taking in his strong, handsome features. Her gaze traced the lines of his generous mouth.

"Lady Tempest," he said, pointedly. "I believe ye wish to tell me something."

She met his gaze, his blue eyes penetrating. Her stomach fluttered. She licked her dry lips, then cleared her throat. "I just...I don't understand why things have become so different between us."

He shrugged his shoulders. "I see no difference."

She stiffened, choking back her anger at his denial. Clearing her throat, she continued, "When ye first arrived at Castle Bron, ye were kind to me. I...I thought..."

"Ye thought what?"

His impatient tone made her temper flare. "I thought ye cared about me," she snapped. Then she closed her eyes and took a deep breath. "What I meant to say is that there have been moments shared between us that ye cannot deny."

He arched a brow at her. "I can and I do."

Her nostrils flared. "How can ye say that?" She pressed her hand to her heart. "I have felt yer desire for me, Caleb. I've seen it in yer eyes."

Brows drawn, he sat up. "Ye know naught of what ye speak. Go back to bed like a good wee lass before ye get hurt."

She lifted her chin defiantly. "Ye would never hurt me."

His gaze did not waver. "Are ye so certain of that?" he replied, his voice deadly soft. "There is much ye don't know about me."

The warning in his tone made a shiver shoot up her spine, but she spoke with quiet firmness. "I am certain. Ye're a gentleman."

He stood abruptly and closed the distance between them in two strides. "Ye're wrong, my lady." He crushed her against his chest. "I'm a lowly born scoundrel." He bent her back and seized her lips in a harsh kiss. Struggling, she pushed against his chest as she fought to pry her lips free from his.

But then his kiss softened.

His crushing hold on her melted into an embrace, warm and close. He stroked his hand down her waist. A soft moan escaped her lips, but he stiffened at the sound and jerked her upright, then set her away from him.

His chest heaved. Anger lit his eyes. "Go back to yer castle."

Heart racing, her body on fire, she shook her head. "But—"

His eyes narrowed on her, cold and hard. "Enough," he snapped. "Ye mean nothing to me. Crawl into yer warm bed and forget about the moments ye've tricked yerself into believing we have shared."

Tears flooded her blue eyes as she scurried to the ladder and climbed down. Her hands shook as she clung to the rungs.

When she reached the bottom, she glared up at him, anger coursing through her veins. "If I never again set eyes on ye, it will be too soon." Then she turned and fled the stables.

She kept her tears in check, until she closed her chamber door behind her. Burying her face in her pillow, she gave vent to her heartache. Tears streamed down her cheeks. The memory of his mocking tone blasted her mind. She rolled onto her side and felt her mouth. Her lips were tender and bruised from his kiss...a kiss that meant nothing to him.

By his own words, *she* meant nothing to him.

With a huff, she stood up and crossed the room to where her trunk sat in the corner. Seizing it, she set it on the bed and threw open the lid. From within her wardrobe, she pulled several tunics off their pegs and tossed them unceremoniously into it, then surveyed her quick packing job with satisfaction.

Nothing was holding her back now. She would leave Castle Bron and journey north to Campbell territory to join her sister and Nathan.

Just the idea made her racing heart begin to calm. What she needed was an adventure. New sights and new friends would soon force her more recent preoccupations to fade into dull memory, and she could forget all about the lowly born scoundrel and his cold, unfeeling heart.

Chapter Four

Caleb lay on his pallet long after the sun broke over the horizon. Scrubbing a hand over his face, he blew out a long breath as memories from the previous night bombarded his mind. What had Tempest been thinking, coming to him in the middle of the night, dressed in naught but a thin nightdress that left little to the imagination? Once again, the memory of her unbound pert breasts, full and proud, draped in the soft fabric came to the fore of his thoughts. With a groan, he jumped to his feet and raked his hand through his hair. How could she be so naive? Then again, how could he have behaved so impulsively?

He groaned aloud again but not from desire. Awash in regret, his thoughts returned to the kiss he'd stolen. Wanting to teach her a lesson about the risks of waking men while scantily clad, he had seized her in a crushing embrace to prove the simple point that she had, once again, put herself in danger.

But he hadn't counted on losing control.

He closed his eyes as he remembered the feel of her full lips pressed against his and the sweetness of her taste.

"Damnation," he cursed as his body responded to the memory of touching her silken skin.

The truth he so adamantly denied was that he had wanted Lady Tempest from the very moment they met. He couldn't help but be drawn to her dazzling appeal and infectious smile. Still, he was no stranger to beautiful women. What set Lady Tempest apart from many of her sex was her intrepid spirit, which he could not help but admire. Her courage and heart were unmatched. Sure, she was reckless and quick-tempered now, but he knew, in time, she would come to find the wisdom in restraint.

A smile played at his lips when he imagined Lady Tempest as she was destined to be one day—bold, passionate, and kind. A true queen.

His smile faltered.

A queen who would no doubt marry a laird.

Taking a deep breath, he resolved, once again, to push the lady from his thoughts—something he had been struggling to do since he arrived at Castle Bron. He had even tried distancing himself from the youngest Brodie lady by choosing to sleep in the stables rather than accepting one of the guest chambers in the castle. What he hadn't counted on was how much time Lady Tempest among the horses. An avid rider, she groomed Storm herself. More than that, she regularly helped Jacob with his chores and sought out Arthur to teach her the finer points of running the stables.

And despite his denials, they had, indeed, shared moments...breaths of intimacy when their eyes had locked and—

"Enough," he said out loud, willing himself to forget.

It had been weeks since he had felt the heat of her desire. In fact, as soon as he recognized that she seemed to be equally drawn to him, he had been doing everything within his power to stem the tide of their burgeoning attraction, including avoiding her company at all costs.

"Damn ye, Nathan," he muttered as he began to pace back and forth.

Caleb shouldn't even be at Castle Bron, and had it not been for Nathan's request that he personally safeguard Lady Tempest, he would have been back in Edinburgh assembling a new gang of bounty hunters, or, with the small fortune he had already amassed, he might have retired and gone west to find a quiet isle to live out his days, alone.

Struck by a sudden realization, he drew to an abrupt halt.

After last night, was he still the best man to protect her?

He remembered the hurt in her tear-filled eyes as she had fled from the stables, her lips bruised from his stolen kiss.

What seemed undeniable at that moment was that the greatest immediate threat to Tempest's safety and happiness was not Clan Brodie's ruthless neighbor, Laird MacKintosh...it was Caleb.

His continued presence only encouraged her affection, although after last night, he was certain he had earned her animosity. A part of him regretted this, but he knew it was for the best. He had no right to her heart. She deserved a better man than he—a laird who could give her the life she truly wanted, surrounded by family and joy, neither of which Caleb could offer her.

With renewed purpose, he rolled up his pallet and collected his saddle bags. Then, he climbed down from the loft and readied his mount. With a last look at the Brodie stables, he made a brief stop in the kitchen before he swung up on his horse and set out for the training fields where he knew Declan was likely running drills with the Brodie warriors.

When the older man spied Caleb's approach, he gestured to his second, Nachlan, to take over the exercises. Nachlan was a shrewd warrior. His long hair was as bright as fire, which he wore in several thick plaits down his back. While the ginger-haired warrior stepped from the ranks to face the assembly of Brodie fighters, Declan turned an expectant gaze on Caleb.

"Good morrow," Declan said with a smile. "'Tis not often ye seek out my company. Usually, I have to track ye down to exchange even the simplest pleasantries."

Caleb managed a slight smile. "I've not come to exchange pleasantries. I've come to say goodbye."

"Ye're leaving? But ye told our laird that ye would stay on until his return."

Caleb nodded. "I did, but circumstances have changed. I've decided I can serve Clan Brodie best by leaving."

Declan gave Caleb an assessing look. "I wish ye'd stay, but ye're yer own man. Ye can come and go as ye like. When were ye thinking of leaving?"

"Immediately."

Declan's eyes widened. "So soon?"

Caleb nodded. "Agnes gave me some dried meat and bannock for the journey. My thanks for the provisions."

Declan reached out and placed his hand on Caleb's shoulder. "Of course, my friend. Ye've served Clan Brodie well and for that ye have my gratitude. Please know that ye're always welcome here."

Caleb dipped his head respectfully. "Thank ye."

Declan smiled. "Go with God. And fear not, for I shall ensure Lady Tempest's safety myself."

"I know ye will, and I've no doubt that ye're better suited to the task than I."

"That I'm not so sure about. 'Tis interesting..." Declan began but his words trailed off.

Caleb cocked a brow at him. "What's interesting?"

Declan shrugged. "Lady Tempest has decided to leave Castle Bron as well."

Caleb stiffened. "What?"

"Aye, she spoke with Murray and me just this morrow. She leaves in three days' time on Saint Columba Day when Laird MacKintosh is certain to be occupied with his clan's festivities. Of course, Tempest is disappointed to miss our own feast and games. Still, she knows we must take advantage of the distraction to ensure her safe passage through MacKintosh lands."

Caleb clenched his fists.

Just when he thought he had finally found a way to put some distance between himself and the clan's unwed lady, she had decided to leave Brodie territory.

He turned away, cursing under his breath. No doubt her sudden desire to flee Castle Bron was because of his own rash impulse to kiss her the night before.

Declan's news changed everything.

While Tempest remained at Castle Bron, she might have been better off without him there, but now that she planned to leave the safety of her kin and cross through enemy territory, not only would Nathan and Elora never forgive him for leaving—but he would also never forgive himself should any harm befall her.

Turning back around, he met Declan's gaze. "I will join her escort through MacKintosh lands."

Without waiting for a reply, he swung up on his horse and rode away from the training fields toward the gates of Castle Bron, gates he had thought he would never pass through again. Steeling his shoulders, he resigned himself, once again, to suffer the temptation of Lady Tempest's company, but only until they made it through enemy territory. As soon as they cleared the boundaries of Clan MacKintosh, he would set out on his own. Having suppressed his attraction to her for several weeks, he could handle a few more days. Still, doubtless, the torture would be acute—for now he knew the taste of her full lips and the feel of her soft curves, melting in his arms.

Chapter Five

Tempest sat with Agnes and Alison at the table in the kitchen. Agnes's ruddy face was redder than usual from the exertions of preparing for the day's feast.

Alison reached across the table. "I can't believe ye're leaving today of all days. 'Tis Saint Columba Day."

Tempest leaned over and kissed Alison on the cheek. "I would have preferred to leave on the morrow, but Declan and Murray insisted on today."

Agnes's brow pinched with worry. "I wish ye'd reconsider leaving, and I'm not alone. Firtha is heartsick with worry."

A slight smile curved Tempest's lips. "Firtha is always worried." She blew out a slow breath. "I ken ye want me to stay, but..." Her words trailed off. She couldn't tell Agnes that she was leaving to separate herself from the withdrawn and disagreeable, yet irresistibly sexy man who slept in the stables.

Once again, Caleb intruded upon her thoughts as memories from three nights past came unbidden to her mind—the way her heart had raced when he seized her in a crushing embrace, the shock and fear that filled her as his lips harshly claimed hers, and then the sudden shift when his touch softened and his kiss deepened and the stables melted away...

Tempest stiffened in her seat and cleared her throat, forcing her mind out of the stables and back to the kitchen. "I just have to go," she blurted.

Alison reached across the table and squeezed her hand. "Ye're restless. I ken. And ye're unhappy." She patted her hand lovingly. "As I've always told yer sister, ye're a spirited lass, my lady. I will miss ye, but I am glad for ye."

Tempest smiled. "Thank ye, Alison. I'm excited. I've never been so far from home."

Declan appeared at the kitchen door. "My lady," he said, drawing her gaze. "'Tis time."

Tempest nodded and pressed a kiss first to Agnes's ruddy cheek and then to Alison's dimpled one. "I will miss ye both."

"Ye be careful," Agnes admonished, giving Tempest a pointed look. "Mind yer temper."

"Don't do anything rash," Alison chimed in.

Tempest nodded. "I'll try. I promise."

She knew she was doing the right thing. The sooner she was away from Caleb the better. Within the boundaries of Clan Campbell and with the support of Elora, she would forget all about Caleb and find new purpose for herself.

She followed Declan out into the courtyard where Storm, a band of Brodie warriors, and Murray, the Steward of Castle Bron, awaited her.

Murray's long silver plait fell over his shoulder when he bowed at her approach. Then he straightened and vowed, "My lady, please know that I will care for Clan Brodie in yer absence."

Tempest rose up on her toes to press a kiss to Murray's cheek. "I know ye will. When our lady and laird left, they bade me come with them, assuring me that our people would thrive in yer capable hands."

Murray's expression grew serious. In a low voice, he said, "I've watched ye of late. The only time I've glimpsed yer smile has been at a distance when I've seen ye riding." He cupped her cheek. "Go now. Join yer sister's company. I will pray that ye find yer smile."

Tempest forced her lips to curve. "Ye needn't wait for my return to see me smile."

Murray's eyes shone with warmth. He clasped her hands. "Thank ye for humoring an old man, but I was one of the blessed few to have had the pleasure of holding ye as a wee bairn. I know when yer smiles are real."

"Rest assured," she said squeezing his hands. "I think this adventure is the balm my soul needs."

"Promise me one thing, my lady," Murray said quickly, releasing her hands.

She nodded. "Anything."

"Remember to listen to the soft voices in yer mind. The quietest voices are always angels. They'll guide ye. And heed Declan and the other guards. And mind ye don't do anything—"

"Reckless," she finished for him. "I ken. I've already promised Agnes and Alison, not to mention Elora and Nathan before they left." She squeezed his hand. "I promise to try."

Without Caleb in her life, she felt confident that she at least had a chance at keeping her word to her kin. She crossed to Storm's side where Arthur awaited her.

"My lady," he said as he bent low and threaded his fingers.

"Thank ye, Arthur," she replied and placed her slippered foot in his hands. With a bounce, she mounted Storm. Her beloved horse whinnied, then stomped at the ground.

Arthur smiled. "She senses the adventure to come and is as eager as her mistress."

Declan pulled his mount alongside Storm. "Are ye ready, my lady?"

Tempest scanned the smiling faces of her kinfolk who had ceased preparations for the day's celebration to see her off. She shifted in her saddle, her gaze searching the courtyard until she realized that she was looking for wavy black hair, clear blue eyes, and broad shoulders. Straightening her back, she lifted her chin in defiance against her own treacherous thoughts and looked straight ahead at the open gate.

It mattered not that Caleb wasn't among those gathered to bid her farewell. In fact, his absence at her departure only proved what his own actions had demonstrated—he didn't care about her. She lifted her chin higher as she silently vowed never again to allow her attraction to a man to guide her choices. Before she'd met Caleb, she had never given much thought to love or marriage. What she had always wanted more than anything was a purpose—to feel necessary and useful to her clan.

Declan leaned close and softly asked, "Were ye looking for someone in particular?"

"Of course not," she lied. Then she cleared her throat. "I was actually just thinking about how I would like to begin formal training under Arthur when I return."

Declan's eyes widened. "And toward what purpose."

She looked him straight on. "To be stablemaster one day, of course."

Declan chuckled. "Ye're a spirited lass to be sure." He lifted his shoulders. "When we reach Campbell lands, ye can ask yer sister for her blessing." He leaned across the space between them and squeezed her hand reassuringly. "For now, I wish to clear MacKintosh land as soon as possible so that we can enjoy this first long journey of yers." He took up his reins. "Let's ride!"

Feeling a rush of excitement, a smile broke across her face. Then she called out to her kin. "Farewell! I shall see ye all again soon!" Her gaze settled on Firtha who was crying into Alison's shoulder. "It will be all right, Firtha," she called to her distraught maid. "I'll remember all ye've taught me."

Tempest's reassurance brought a brave smile to Firtha's lips while she continued to weep, forcing her pinched features into an oddly pained yet joyful looking expression.

Giving a final wave to her kinfolk, Tempest nudged Storm forward and followed Declan through the castle gates. The villagers lined the roadside as they passed by. Tempest waved and smiled. Then a sudden pang struck her heart. She was leaving home for the first time. But as the village and Castle Bron receded in the distance her excitement began to build again. She breathed deep the fresh summer air, tasting freedom on the wind.

"I'm going to ride ahead," she said to Declan before driving her heels into Storm's flanks. The thrill of the ride coursed through her. She shot forward, passing the other guards. Wind whipped through her unbound hair. Smiling, she raised her face to the soft morning sun. For the first time in many weeks, she felt the promise of new beginnings. With so much to look forward to, it was all she could do to contain her excitement, but she eventually reined in her mount and rode alongside Declan.

"Tell me whose lands we must pass through," she asked.

The seasoned captain scratched at his silver stubble. "Och, let me see. MacKintosh, of course, the scoundrels, and then

Fraser, MacKenzie, and Munro. Clan Campbell is north of Munro territory."

"What about Inverness? Will we pass through Inverness?" she asked eagerly.

Declan shook his head. "Nay, lass, we'll go around. Inverness will be overrun with pilgrims and other travelers. Remember, today is Saint Columba Day."

"I'm sorry to hear that."

He smiled reassuringly. "Mayhap on our return journey, we'll pass through Inverness."

"Declan, that would be wonderful," she exclaimed.

~ * ~

When the sun had risen higher in the sky, Tempest grew tired of the steady pace and, once again, nudged her horse to speed up. Bending low in the saddle, she urged Storm to race faster over the purple moors, but an instant later, she jerked on the reins. A rider had crested the hill in front of her. Bringing Storm to a halt, she shielded her eyes from the sun, which shown brightly behind the mounted figure, casting the person in shadow. Fearing he was a MacKintosh scout, she started to turn Storm around, but then a cloud shifted, blotting out the sun.

Her stomach dropped out. "Nay," she whispered, recognizing Caleb astride his black horse. Her heart pounded as he drew close. "What are ye doing here?" she demanded.

His face showed no emotion as he drew to a halt beside her. "I was scouting the road ahead," he replied before nudging his horse forward. She reached out and grabbed his reins, forcing him to stop. "Ye know very well what I was asking," she hissed. "Why are ye here?"

He met her gaze. "I promised Nathan that I would protect ye. I will ensure that ye make it through MacKintosh land safely."

She dropped his reins and tossed her hair over her shoulder, lifting her chin defiantly. "I don't need yer escort. I have Declan and Nachlan and a dozen Brodie warriors."

He did not reply. With a shrug of his shoulders, he clicked his tongue, urging his mount into a trot toward Declan. Fury pulsed through her as she watched the captain of the Brodie guard welcome Caleb with a smile. Choking back a screech of frustration, she jerked her horse around and rode to meet them.

"Ye didn't tell me that ye asked Caleb to join our party," she said accusingly to Declan.

Declan raised his brows. "Given our current feud with our neighbor, I told ye that I would assemble the strongest escort I could."

She raked a hand through her unbound curls. "I assumed ye meant Brodie warriors."

"Caleb has been given a place within our clan, not just because of his partnership with our laird, but he is also favored by yer sister and respected by our kinfolk."

"Aye, he's a saint," she scoffed, shooting a fierce gaze at the man in question. His expression remained impassive, which only fueled her anger. But more than his cool indifference, the betrayal of her body at his closeness pushed her fury to new heights. Desire fluttered in her stomach as the memory of their passionate kiss assailed her thoughts.

Swallowing a string of curses, she jerked her mount around and rode ahead.

"How is this happening?" she fumed to herself.

Just when she thought she was finally free of Caleb, he rode back into her life. She shot a defiant look over her shoulder—he may be a member of her escort, but that didn't mean that she needed to stay close to him.

Driving her heels into Storm's flanks, she broke into a gallop, giving herself over to the ride. The power of Storm's stride and the speed at which they raced made her heart pound. In that moment, she was no longer a maid with a broken heart—she and Storm were one. And together, they were the wind that barreled across the moors and the sun that warmed the lush earth. Closing her eyes, she savored the moment. But then she heard the pounding of hooves behind her. Shifting in her saddle, she glanced back. Brow furrowed, Caleb thundered toward her.

She knew that look of disapproval.

She had seen the same expression many times—on her sister's face, Declan's, Murray's, Firtha's, and even Alison's. A feeling of foreboding swept over her as she reined in her horse.

"What have I done now?" she snapped.

Caleb reached out and seized her reins. "Ye must slow yer pace," he admonished her. "Yer reckless speed not only places yer own life in danger, but it also endangers the lives of yer men by making it harder for them to protect ye."

"Give me back the reins!"

"I'm not finished," he said firmly. "Ye've given no thought to Storm's wellbeing. We've significant ground to cover this day, and yet ye're going to run yer mount ragged."

Her face burned. She had not meant to be reckless or thoughtless. She had only wanted to get away from him, which was the purpose of her leaving Castle Bron in the first place.

"I will slow down," she replied stiffly.

"I'm still not finished," he said, his tone even, but she could feel his anger. "The din of yer horse's hooves can be heard for a great distance. We're about to cross into enemy lands. Ye may have already alerted MacKintosh scouts to our presence."

She winced, casting her gaze to the ground. "I didn't realize," she muttered. Then, taking a deep breath, she, once more, met his gaze. "I will stay close and slow my pace."

"Ye will align yer horse with Declan's."

She frowned. "Ye needn't scold me like a petulant child. I will heed yer council and stay close."

"Ye will align yer horse with Declan's, or else I'll lift ye off that horse and onto my own," he said pointedly.

"How dare ye—" she started to say, her voice rising, but then he moved closer. "If ye continue to protest, I'm going to assume it is because ye wish to ride with me."

She glared at him before she turned her horse around and trotted back to Declan's side.

"Forgive me," she said to the captain. "I did not mean to cause trouble."

"I ken ye meant no harm," Declan said. "We'll manage. That I do not doubt."

Taking a deep breath, she resolved to follow Firtha's most frequently uttered advice...*Slow down. Think things through.*

Her chest tightened as she shifted her gaze forward. Caleb led the way. Her gaze traced the breadth of his shoulders and then his well-muscled legs, which were bare beneath the Brodie plaid he wore. She fought to hold onto her anger, but her fury soon gave way to confusion and regret. Whether it drifted to her on the wind or by memory, his scent came to her. Then the feel of his strong arms holding her close and the taste of his kiss. She closed her eyes against the longing that flooded her heart.

Why couldn't he have just stayed away?

Opening her eyes, her gaze once again settled on his strong shoulders. How many nights had she lain awake dreaming about loving him and being loved in return?

Too many.

Her knuckles whitened from gripping her reins so tightly. She knew she needed to stop caring for him.

But how could she when he was so damn close?

Chapter Six

Caleb rode in lead for some time, allowing both his frustration and his desire to cool. He detested having to be so cold to Tempest. It went against his nature, but it was his duty to protect her—from Egan, from himself, and even from her own desire. Expelling a heavy breath, he tried as much as possible to keep his thoughts trained on the task ahead—leading the party safely through MacKintosh lands. Then, he would go his separate way.

"Caleb," Declan called from behind.

Caleb glanced back, his gaze settling first on the captain, but then shifting involuntarily to the raven-haired beauty at his side. Taking a fortifying breath, he motioned to Nachlan to take lead before turning his horse around and trotting back to meet Declan.

"Aye," Caleb answered when he drew his horse alongside the captain's.

Declan scrubbed a hand over his face. "If we keep to the open road, we'll make better time, although we do run the risk of being spotted by scouts. Still, their number is certain to be fewer because of the feast. Otherwise, we can pass through the wood yonder," he said pointing to a dense forest edge in the distance. "The road follows close to the river. It will be slow going, but I expect our chances of being seen are slimmer."

"Where do ye plan to bed down tonight? Inverness?"

"Nay, we ride for Frasier territory. Inverness is certain to be overrun with travelers."

"Ye ask as if yer not coming with us," Tempest chimed in.

He had hoped to avoid speaking with her. Shifting his gaze to meet her lovely blue eyes, he said, "I'm not taking ye all the way to Campbell territory. As soon as ye're safely through MacKintosh lands, I'm going my own way."

A fleeting but unmistakable look of pain crossed her face before she turned away, shifting her gaze to the sloping moors.

Caleb steeled his heart against the regret that threatened to weaken his resolve. Taking a deep breath, he turned back to Declan. "Let us take the forest path. I will tell Nachlan." He glanced at Tempest. Her exquisite profile held an impassive expression. His chest tightened as he urged his horse forward, once again taking lead.

~ * ~

The silence of the cool, dense forest was broken only by the sound of splintering branches and rustling leaves beneath the clomping of their horses' hooves. In the distance, Caleb could hear the rushing river and occasionally the path wound close enough so that they glimpsed the flowing currents. He rode side by side with Nachlan who, like Caleb, was a man of few words. Both sat alert in their saddles while scanning the trees for danger.

"How much further now?" Caleb asked Nachlan in a low voice.

"We're well over halfway to Frasier land. 'Tis not far now."

Caleb nodded. "Soon," he murmured to himself.

Suddenly, he stiffened and raised his fist, signaling to the men and woman behind him to halt. Nachlan shot him a questioning glance. Caleb motioned for him to remain silent. They both gently urged their horses forward, scanning the trees for movement, but all was quiet. The tension began to ease from Caleb's shoulders, but then he heard a horse whinny ahead of them. An instant later, a rider clad in the MacKintosh plaid broke through the trees onto the path, racing away from them. And behind him, came a second rider.

"MacKintosh scouts," Nachlan hissed. "They've seen us!" Nachlan raised his crossbow, taking aim at the rider in the rear.

"Ye kill him and ye start a war," Caleb snapped.

"Blast!" Nachlan lowered his weapon. "Ye're right." He turned and met Caleb's gaze. "I couldn't have shot a fleeing man in the back anyway. Still, with the size of our party, they'll be able to track us for sure."

Declan pulled his horse alongside Caleb's. "I've no doubt Egan will send a band of warriors after us." He blew out a long breath. "We will be outnumbered." Then his gaze shifted to where Tempest sat astride her mount. "And they will take our lady."

Her face went ashen. "This is all my fault. Had I been more cautious earlier—"

Caleb shook his head. "Ye're not at fault, my lady. Egan's ruthless character is to blame. Ye did not start this feud."

"What is our course now?" Nachlan asked.

Caleb met Declan's gaze. He could see the worry etched on the older man's face. Taking a deep breath, Caleb did what he knew he must. "Lady Tempest and I will separate from the party."

Nachlan shook his head. "They'll see yer tracks and know that we've split up, except that ye will not stand a chance against a band of warriors."

"Not if they go on foot and follow the River Findhorn," Declan said, hope brightening his eyes. "The river leads into the Firth of Moray. Ye'll be able to take a ferry into the harbor of Inverness."

Caleb nodded with grim resolve.

"But Declan, what will ye do? " Tempest asked, her brow drawn.

"Do not fash yerself about the rest of us, my lady," Declan began, "If we ride hard and our horses don't give out, we can make it to Frasier land before they catch up to us."

Tempest's nostrils flared as she looked beseechingly at Declan. "Ye know I can ride as well as any man here. Let us stay together!"

"Tempest," Caleb said, drawing her gaze. "'Tis too risky."

Declan nodded. "Yer safety comes first, my lady." Then he shifted his gaze to meet Caleb's. "Follow the river to Inverness. We will meet at the livery near the cathedral."

"When?" Tempest asked.

"As soon as we're able, my lady," Declan said gently.

Caleb swung down from his mount, crossed to where Tempest sat astride her horse, and reached for her. But she shook her head. Tears stung her eyes. "I don't want to separate, and I don't want to leave Storm."

"Ye needn't worry," he reassured her. "Declan and the others will take care of her."

"We will protect her," Declan vowed.

"We promise," Nachlan echoed.

Caleb grasped her waist. Hesitantly, she placed her hands on his shoulders, and he lifted her down. His chest tightened as he met her worried gaze.

"I am so sorry, Caleb," she whispered.

He could see the sincerity in her eyes and knew she blamed herself for the trouble they'd encountered. "Ye did not intentionally commit any wrongdoing." He lifted his shoulders. "We do not know if they followed us into the wood or if they were already here patrolling for tinkers. For all we know, the blame could fall on my shoulders for having chosen this route."

Regret shadowed her face. "'Twas my own folly to have set out from Castle Bron to begin with."

"Nay, my lady," Caleb said firmly. "Ye're not to be imprisoned in yer own keep. Ye have every right to travel to Campbell lands to be with yer sister. Egan is not our master. If we allow the threat he represents to dictate our actions, then he wins. Do ye understand?"

She took a tremulous breath and nodded.

"Our destination is still the same. 'Tis only our course and the method of reaching our destination that has changed."

"*Our* destination?" she asked softly.

He nodded. "It looks like I'm going with ye at least until Inverness. Now," he began, taking a step back, "I ken ye'll want to say goodbye, but remember, 'tis only for a brief time."

She took a deep breath and straightened her shoulders. Then she turned to Storm and pressed her cheek to her muzzle. She stroked the chestnut mare's black mane and crooned gentle words indiscernible to Caleb's ears, but her sorrow was clear.

After several moments passed, he stepped forward and gently clasped her arm. "We must away, all of us."

She nodded and took a step before turning to face Declan. "Ride swiftly," she bade him.

"We will, my lady. And worry naught. I will meet ye in Inverness. Ye have my word."

"Go with God," Caleb said to Declan.

The older man nodded resolutely. "And ye." He drove his heels into his horse's flanks, pulling Storm behind him. "Let's ride, men!"

Caleb could feel Tempest tremble as her warriors rode away. When they were alone, he turned to face her. "Come," he said softly. But then he noticed the tears still flooding her eyes. As much as he wanted to protect his own heart, he could not do so at the expense of hers. He opened his arms. "Ye're not a mountain. Ye're a flesh and blood woman, and a young one at that. Let go yer tears."

She covered her mouth with her hand as his words freed her emotions. He folded her in his arms. Her hand grasped his tunic. She shook gently as she cried silent tears against his chest. He breathed deep her scent, and for a moment, he allowed the tension to release from his shoulders. He held her tightly, savoring her closeness. With her in his arms, it felt like coming home.

He closed his eyes against the bitterness that suddenly rose in his heart at his own thought.

He had never had a real home. He swallowed hard as he drew away and met her gaze. "We shouldn't delay any longer."

She nodded, swiping at her cheeks.

Taking her hand, he started to lead her toward the river.

"Blast," he whispered under his breath.

Now, it was just him and Tempest...alone...in the woods.

"Caleb," she said.

He glanced back and met her deep blue eyes. Her porcelain skin was pink from her tears. "I truly am sorry."

"As am I," he breathed.

Facing forward, his jaw tensed, and his nostrils flared as the intimacy of the present struck him to his core. "As am I."

For so long he had stayed away from her only to suddenly be thrust together.

He took a deep breath. He had always prided himself on being a man of strong will.

But there were limits to anyone's self-control.

Chapter Seven

Weeks ago, even days ago, Tempest would have given anything to suddenly have no choice but to be alone with Caleb. In fact, she had longed for that very thing. But now...now she wasn't certain what she wanted.

Biting her lip, she eyed the man walking in front of her. Her gaze trailed over his broad shoulders, down his arm to his hand, which clutched hers protectively. Watching him, rather than the path, her foot caught on a branch. He turned quickly and pulled her close, catching her fall.

Breathless, she met his gaze.

"Are ye all right?" he asked, his brow drawn with concern.

Heart racing, she nodded. His hand lingered at her waist. For a moment, heat filled his gaze, making her stomach flutter. But then he cleared his throat, and his expression became impassive once more. "Shall we continue?"

Again, she nodded, feeling completely tongue-tied as she had often felt in his presence. Turning back to the path, he continued to lead her forward. There was an ease in his bearing and a softness in his voice that she had not seen or heard for some time. His behavior reminded her of when he'd first arrived at Castle Bron—quietly attentive.

Her heart flooded with warmth.

Why was he suddenly being so kind?

But she shook her head, fighting to quell her response to his tender care. She was coming to realize that there were many sides to Caleb. His eyes flashing in anger and his cold, mocking tone were also burned into memory. She took a deep breath as she struggled to keep the shields she had erected around her heart in place. Regardless of his sudden change toward her, he had made his intentions clear. Once they met Declan in Inverness, Caleb would go his separate way.

Taking a deep breath, she forced her thoughts away from his leanly muscular physique and the feel of his strong hand holding hers and took in her surroundings. Tree limbs branched out overhead, their leafy bows casting dancing shadows on the forest floor. The river rippled alongside them. She scanned the water, which glistened in places where beams of light were permitted passage through the dense summer foliage.

He turned suddenly. Worry etched on his brow. "The river is quieter here," he said quickly. Then he swept her into his arms, forcing a squeal of surprise from her lips.

"What are ye doing?" she demanded, her heart thundering in her chest.

"I want to ensure we do not leave our scent behind for Egan's hounds to find," he explained, looking straight on, his face unreadable. Were it not for the pulse ticking rapidly at his throat, she would have believed him to be completely unaffected by their sudden intimacy.

Clutching his tunic, she managed to say, "That seems prudent."

His heart pounded beneath her fist. Incapable of controlling herself, she splayed her fingers wide across his chest, drawn by his heartbeat and warmth. She took a deep breath only to regret what she had hoped would be a calming action as his rich, masculine scent filled her from the inside out.

"Put me down," she blurted

His eyes widened slightly. "Here? But I cannot."

She forced a casual smile to her lips. "Don't be fooled by my surcote. Firtha convinced me to wear it. Ye know I'm not opposed to a getting a little wet and dirty. I don't mind wading through the river."

He shifted his gaze forward. "My brogues are made to release the water. They'll dry quickly."

"Still," she said, feeling as if her heart would surely burst through her skin if she were to stay in his strong embrace for another moment. "I would rather not burden ye with my weight."

He chuckled, surprising her. "Ye're as light as a sack of grain."

So rare was his spontaneous laughter that she couldn't help but smile. They locked eyes. His pace slowed. For a moment, she lost herself in his deep blue gaze. He licked his sensual, firm lips, making her mouth water for his kiss.

Once again, clearing his throat, he shifted his gaze straight on and sloshed through the river at an almost desperate pace. After several torturous moments passed, he crossed to the other side, carried her through the thick bracken and bushes at the water's edge, then abruptly set her feet down on the forest floor.

Both relief and regret filled her as his hands left her body. He stood stiffly. A scowl shadowed his face. Without a word, he took her hand, but despite the hardness of his expression, his touch remained tender. Her stomach fluttered as he led her through the trees. So intent was her gaze on his broad back that she did not notice when they'd left the forest behind; that is, until he came to an abrupt halt.

Shifting her gaze, she gasped. Only a few strides in front of them loomed a narrow, rocky ledge.

"Tis the Firth of Moray," he said, leaning to peer over the edge. "It opens to the harbor. If we follow it, we shall reach Inverness."

She stepped past him, boldly looking down at the swiftly moving river. "How do ye propose we get down?"

He pulled her back from the edge. "Not from here," he said, giving her a suspicious look. Then he cleared his throat in a way that reminded her of Murray or Declan when they were about to address what they might perceive as her less than ladylike behavior. She stiffened, knowing what was coming next.

"My lady," Caleb began, "while ye're under my protection, please do not do anything—"

"Rash, reckless?" she said, finishing his sentence for him. "I wasn't planning on jumping or scaling down the cliffside, if that is yer worry."

His eyes narrowed on her. "Do ye promise?"

She glanced pointedly down at what would surely be a fatal drop. "I may be a wee bit bold for a lady, but I'm not mad."

Seemingly convinced, he let go of her hand and scanned the ridge. Then he pointed across to the other side of the firth, where, further upstream, a plume of smoke coiled up to the sky. "I'd wager 'tis a croft."

Once more taking her hand, he began to follow the ridge line. "There must be a way down," he said absently. They carried on until the smoke was opposite them.

"I thought as much," he said.

She followed his gaze to a skiff tied on the bank and a dirt path that cut through the trees. "But how do we get to it," she asked.

"There," he exclaimed, pointing ahead to where the cliff began to dip lower. He kept a firm grip on her hand as he hastened forward. Soon, they reached a place where the face of the cliff was not as steep but was, instead, comprised of jutting rocks and boulders, allowing them to pick their way down. Caleb bade her wait while he jumped from the last rock. Then he turned and reached for her.

Her chest tightened at the sight of his open arms. How many times had she dreamed of filling his embrace? "I can manage on my own," she said stiffly.

"Ordinarily, I wouldn't doubt ye, but ye're wearing more than usual."

She pulled at her confining surcote and thin cloak. "I told Firtha it was impractical to wear all this," she muttered while considering the drop. It wasn't so very far down, but her knees could not fully bend in the stiff fabric. "Ye're right," she admitted and leaned down, placing her hands on his shoulders. Once more, their eyes locked. He clasped her beneath the arms, his gaze never leaving hers.

Time seemed to stop. She felt like a feather slowly drifting toward the ground. Her body grazed his. She fought against the desire to entwine her arms around his neck. A smile, fleeting but undeniable curved his kissable mouth, and then her feet landed on solid earth.

Once again, he released her quickly and took a step back.

Taking a deep breath, she pressed her hands to her warm cheeks while he began sifting through his saddle bags.

"What is that for?" she asked when he withdrew several silver pieces from a sack of coin.

He jerked his head toward the other side of the firth. "We need that skiff to get to Inverness."

"Surely, that amount would buy a dozen skiffs. Mayhap they will sell it for less."

"I don't plan on asking. So, this is payment for the skiff and the inconvenience of me taking it without notice." He turned to face her, giving her an appraising look. "We'll have to wade across. I'm afraid 'tis too deep for me to spare ye the unpleasantness of getting wet. I'm going to hold my saddle bags on my shoulders to keep them dry. Ye might wish to remove a layer or two so that ye're not too weighed down."

She fingered her thin cloak, wondering if it was wise to undress even a little while alone in the woods with Caleb. "What are ye going to take off?"

"Nothing," he answered.

"Not even yer tunic?"

"Nay."

"I don't understand why ye wear a tunic in fine weather. If I were a man, I wouldn't."

He only shrugged in reply.

"Nothing would give me greater pleasure than to wear a plaid and a pair of brogues." She sighed. "I suppose I will have to settle for removing this cage." She tugged at her fitted surcote. "I did promise Firtha that I would keep it on while I traveled, but then again, our trip has certainly not gone as planned." She untied her cloak, letting it fall to the ground. "I feel better already." Then she turned around, showing her back to Caleb. "Ye'll have to help me with the laces."

She piled her thick curly hair onto her head, holding it in place with her hands so that Caleb could easily access the ties. Several moments passed. She waited breathlessly to feel his touch. Swallowing hard, she glanced back. He stood so close, staring down at her, his hands fisted at his sides.

"Turn back around," he rasped.

She whirled around, her heart pounding harder than ever. She could feel him draw closer still. His breath warmed her neck, causing a shiver to shoot up her spine. Gently, he tugged at the knot. Her breaths quickened, overcome by the intimacy of being undressed by his hand.

He loosened the laces. Her surcote slipped down to her feet, and for a moment, a breath, his hand rested at her waist. She turned, meeting his gaze. His blue eyes glinted with the same hunger that coursed through her.

"Caleb," she whispered, her hands aching to spread across his chest.

A shadow crossed his face. He jerked around, showing his back to her.

Her brow furrowed. "Caleb?"

He turned to face her. Anger flashed in his gaze. "What do ye want, my lady?" he snapped, his voice hard.

The pit of her stomach twisted while a hollowness settled in her chest. She stiffened. How could she have let down her guard? She was nothing more than a simpering fool. With only a few gentle words and kind deeds, she had, once again, become a lovesick maid. Steeling her shoulders, she held her head high. "Nothing," she said flatly. "I want nothing from ye."

Folding up her surcote, she placed it within her cloak and tied the ends together in a bundle. Then she stepped into the water, and without a backward glance at Caleb, she waded toward the skiff. The water was freezing, sending icy chills to wash away the heat of his touch. She welcomed the cold, wishing that it could penetrate her very soul and forever wash away the unrequited feelings that tortured her heart.

Chapter Eight

Caleb could feel the heat of Tempest's glare on his back, but it was not the same heat that had made her eyes glint with desire. If her gaze could shoot arrows, his back would be a bloody mess—this he did not doubt. Still, he reminded himself that this was as it should be. He should never have softened his manner toward her, but after the run-in with the scouts in the forest he'd had little choice. For the first time, she had appeared truly vulnerable. Something he hadn't even known was possible. Surrendering to instinct, he could not help but soothe away her sorrow. It was his nature to want to protect and reassure her. But his gentle care had allowed his heart to open.

He cursed under his breath, willing his thoughts to remain focused on the task at hand. After all, it was his duty to ensure that she was reunited with Declan, unharmed by him or anyone else.

The brisk wind blew in their favor, sending them scuttling across the choppy waters, straight into the harbor of Inverness. His gaze scanned the busy waterway, using the rudder to direct their small vessel through the maze of merchant ships, skiffs, and crowded ferry boats.

The decision to journey north on Saint Columba Day had been well thought out by Declan and Murray, assuming their path would cut across moors and through forests. But the plan had been to avoid Inverness.

Tension flooded his shoulders when the wharf came into view.

It was mayhem.

Numerous tall ships were anchored in deeper waters, but smaller vessels, too many to count, barreled toward land with little room to maneuver through the crowded port.

He glanced back at Lady Tempest. Much of her hair was wet as was her tunic. It clung to her shapely curves. He noticed then that she had drawn the eye of several sailors.

"Cover yerself with yer cloak," he said, his voice harsher than he had intended.

She glared at him and shook her head. "I think not," she said coolly. "The sun is hot."

His grip tightened on the rudder as he fought for calm. "Aye, but yer tunic is wet."

She shrugged. "It will dry faster in the sun."

He raised his eyes to the Heavens for aid. "Ye're giving these hungry sailors a taste of what they've been missing these last months at sea."

Her cheeks pinkened, but she stiffened her back and tilted her chin. "I don't care. Let them stare. 'Tis they who are rude. I have every right to be here as I am."

His jaw tightened. "Aye," he gritted out. "But 'tis I who will have to fight them should they try to take a closer look."

Her nostrils flared. She flung her hair off her shoulders in defiance, but to his relief, she conceded. "Fine," she said in a clipped tone, and pulled on the cloak, all the while keeping her bearing as noble as a queen's. "Satisfied?" she snapped.

He nodded curtly, then shifted his gaze forward. Spying a gap between several platform ferryboats, he took up a long oar and propelled them forward. After a few near collisions, they reached an opening alongside one of the docks. Seizing his bags, he climbed onto the busy landing, then turned and offered Tempest his hand. She ignored him, tossed her surcote on the dock and hoisted herself up. Smiling victoriously, she stood tall, but then a sailor bumped her as he passed. Her eyes widened. She started to fall back, but Caleb caught her by the waist, keeping her upright.

Eyes locked, they stood like that for a moment, their gazes battling but for what prize he could not say. When it came to each other, there was no winning side.

"Take my hand," he demanded.

"I'm fine," she snapped.

His eyes narrowed. "The wharf is no place for a lady. 'Tis dangerous. Now, take my hand, or I will toss ye over my shoulder."

Her gaze shone with defiance.

He cocked his brow at her. "Do not doubt me," he warned.

Fury reddened her cheeks, but she placed her hand in his. Then he turned and started to move his way through the cramped port. The roads were stifling, crowded as they were with all manner of people—pilgrims, Highlanders, merchants, and vendors. The festivities to honor Saint Columba were underway, and the nearby taverns and brothels overflowed with revelers. Caleb barreled forward, weaving like a snake amid the merrymakers with Tempest in tow. Occasionally, he had to push aside someone too drunk to heed his request to pass, but he did so without hesitation. Now was not the time for social pleasantries. The sooner he could escape the city's more colorful district, the better.

As they moved toward the heart of Inverness, he was astonished by the sheer number of people filling the streets. Whether drawn to the city by holy conviction or mayhem and drink, it was clear that travelers had come from near and far. And all of whom, he realized in that moment, would need a place to bed down for the night.

"Wait," Tempest said suddenly, tugging on his hand.

Stopping, he turned and gave her an expectant look.

"Declan said to meet him at the livery near the cathedral," she began, "Is that not its towers over there."

Looking at where she pointed, he nodded. "Aye, but we need to find rooms for the night. The inns near the cathedral are certain to be full."

She frowned. "But Declan said he would meet us there."

Observing her alarm, he fought his instincts to soothe her. "Declan and the others are riding hard to Frasier territory," he explained. "Their horses will need to rest, which means they will not be able to meet us until the morrow." He started to lead her forward. "Now, come along before all the rooms in Inverness are taken."

Holding tightly to her hand, he pulled her in close behind him, shielding her from merchants shouting offers as they passed by. The noise and chaos blasted his ears. People danced and feasted. Wagons rolled through. Animals scattered underfoot. He glanced back to make sure she was alright, but of course her face shone brightly as she eagerly took in all the sights, smiling at street performers and waving at a cluster of children racing past.

He shook his head at her delight. Other sheltered ladies might have been nervous surrounded by the din of the crowd, but not Tempest. She looked elated.

Finally, they reached an inn with a cleanly swept front stoop and a well fashioned sign. "This will do," he said and pulled her inside. He scanned the common room. The floor appeared to be recently scrubbed, and the serving maids dressed in modest tunics. "Aye," he said again. "This will do nicely."

His gaze settled on a table where an older couple sat studying a ledger. As he approached, they lifted their heads and smiled. Both had white hair and pleasant brown eyes and a flush to their skin that made Caleb think they had also been enjoying some of the festivities.

"Blessings to ye," Caleb said in greeting.

"And to ye," the man said, raising his tankard high.

"Blessings," the woman echoed, joining her husband in taking a long sip from her cup.

"Are ye the keeper of this inn?" Caleb asked.

The man hiccupped. "I am, indeed. How can I help ye?"

Caleb gestured to Tempest. "My lady requires a room for the night, as do I, preferably one adjacent to hers."

He shook his head. "We've fine rooms, to be sure, but we're all full up." Then he glanced at the woman next to him. "Are we not, my dear?"

The innkeeper's wife nodded. "Aye, that we are, to the brim. In fact, we've been full the past fortnight, just like the city. I'm afraid ye won't find a decent room in all of Inverness."

"I'm afraid ye won't find an *indecent* room in all of Inverness," The innkeeper said, before bursting out laughing.

His wife chuckled and swatted him playfully. "Och, William, ye do beat all!"

Caleb dipped his head. "Thank ye for yer...er...help," he said dryly before turning away and pulling Tempest behind him. "There must be a room," he exclaimed, stepping outside.

With purposeful strides, he hastened through the city, stopping at every respectable looking inn or tavern they passed. But each time, they were turned away. He cursed as they stepped back out onto the crowded street.

"What now?" Tempest asked.

He raked a hand through his hair. "The abbey will have more pilgrims than they can handle, I'd wager." He expelled a long breath as he considered their dwindling choices. None were ideal, but he was determined to put some kind of roof over their heads. "Come along," he said resolutely. "We go back to the wharf."

"But I thought ye said that it was dangerous there."

"It is," he replied as he started to lead her back toward the water. "But we've no other choice."

Praying for a miracle that never came, they reached the wharf just as the sun touched down on the horizon, casting a burnished streak through the water. Wanting to get Tempest off the street by nightfall, Caleb began scouring the roadsides, his gaze passing over lively taverns and brothels.

"Do ye think we'll be able to find any rooms?" Tempest asked. Her hesitant tone drew his gaze. As bold as she was, he could tell that she was not unaffected by the raucous scene unfolding before her.

"A single room is all we're looking for now," he said absently while he searched for what he knew did not exist—a respectable brothel. "I will not leave ye alone here for a moment."

She turned to face him. "We are to share a room?"

He nodded grimly. "Aye."

"But we can't," she exclaimed. "We mustn't!"

Just then one of the tavern doors swung wide and two men burst out, their arms entangled in a messy brawl. Caleb gestured to the writhing pair, swinging their fists and gnashing their teeth. "But as ye can see, we have no choice."

Straightening his shoulders, he set his gaze on the sign above the door. It was called The Crescent Moon. "Just pray they have one to spare."

Clasping tightly to her hand, he led her across the street toward the tavern. When they reached the door, he looked at Tempest. "Keep yer head down, and don't look anywhere." He grabbed the latch. "Yer sister is going to kill me," he muttered before he threw open the door.

The common room was teeming with people. Barmaids clad in low-cut bodices wound through the tables, which were heaving with drunken men. Garish laughter filled the room. Breasts were fondled. Patrons jeered and fought. He glanced back at Tempest, whose face was stark white, and could not help but try to soothe her fear. "Everything will be all right. I won't let anything happen to ye."

She squeezed his hand and nodded but did not speak. He drew close. "Look at me," he bade her gently.

She met his gaze. He cupped her cheek. "Keep yer eyes on me," he said softly.

"All right," she breathed.

He led her toward one end of the bar where the keeper was filling tankards of ale. "We need a room," he said loudly over the din of the patrons.

The barkeep looked them both over. "Is it sport ye're after? Another woman to join yer bed?"

Tempest squeezed his hand hard.

"Nay," he said quickly. "My wife and I need a room for the night."

The barkeep shook his head. "We haven't one to spare. I doubt there's a room in all of Inverness."

"What do *ye* know?" a woman said, sauntering up to the barkeep. He swatted her playfully on the rump, and she squealed and scowled at him before a smile broke across her face. Then she turned and leaned sensually over the bar. Her red hair was piled on top of her head while thick ringlets framed what Caleb believed would be a lovely face were it not for all the paint and powders. She reached out and slowly ran her finger down Caleb's cheek. "If ye're willing to pay, I'll give up my room."

"Where will ye sleep?" the barkeep grunted.

She straightened and set her hands on her hips. "If I give Bridget a cut, she'll let me bed down with her." Then she turned and smiled at Caleb. "Bridget's not working until after her wee bairn is born."

"What about ye?" the barkeep protested. "Ye're supposed to be working tonight."

"If he's willing to pay, then I don't mind taking the night off," she declared. "I've spread my legs enough today."

The barkeep scowled down at her. "What about my cut?"

Caleb glanced at Tempest whose eyes were now as round as saucers. He pulled her in front of him, forming a shield around her before letting go of her hand for the first time since they'd set foot on land. Then, he reached into his saddlebags and fished out a handful of coin, which he slapped down on the table. The whore's painted eyes flashed wide at the sight of the silver marks. "We'll take the room!"

She burst out laughing as she scooped up her earnings and dropped the coins down the front of her bodice. "My name's Mary," she said. "Follow me."

Holding tightly to Tempest's hand, Caleb followed Mary up two flights of stairs. Rutting sounds emanated from the doors as they passed. Caleb glanced back at Tempest. Her face had gone from ghostly white to crimson. "This is a bloody nightmare," he muttered to himself.

Finally, Mary stopped and opened one of the doors. Once inside, Caleb scanned the room. The air smelled of musk oil and sex, and the sheets on the bed were mussed.

"We'll need clean linens for the bed, food, and some clean, dry clothing for my wife."

The woman's gaze slowly raked over Tempest from head to toe. "That'll cost ye extra."

Caleb withdrew another mark and handed it to Mary.

Smiling, she slipped the coin into the front of her bodice with the others. "I'll be right back," she said before disappearing out the door.

When they were alone, he turned and looked at Tempest. Her eyes were still wide.

"It will be all right," he assured her again.

The rhythmic sound of a headboard hitting the wall came from the room next to them.

Her eyes widened further still.

He reached for her hand. "'Tis just for the night."

She nodded, her gaze darting about the room uneasily. "I think I should sit down," she said, fanning her face as she moved toward the bed.

"Nay," Caleb blurted, causing her to jump. "Ye don't want to sit there, not yet anyway."

At that moment, Caleb wondered whether sleeping in an alleyway or beneath a stairwell might have been preferable to The Crescent Moon.

Soon, Mary came barreling back into the room. "Here we are," she beamed. "Fresh linens for the bed. A jug of wine and some bread. I found a clean tunic for ye," she said to Caleb. "And Bridget was happy to lend yer wife her nightdress. We'll wash her tunic and set it to dry for the morrow." She paused at the door and slipped a key into the lock. "I recommend keeping the door locked or else ye might have company during the night."

"Thank ye, Mary," Caleb said.

"Thank ye," Tempest echoed.

When the door shut, he turned to Tempest and gave her the nightdress. "Ye change out of yer muddy tunic, and I'll make the bed."

She nodded, accepting the garment.

He set to work, making certain that his back remained to her while she changed. As he made a pile of dirty linens on the floor in the corner and began to spread the clean linen sheet over the straw mattress, he could feel his frustration begin to grow.

How had it come to pass that he was sharing a room with her in a brothel of all places? He suddenly pictured her lying on the bed, her arms open and inviting.

"Nay," he breathed, trying to imagine chaste thoughts.

Attending Mass with Tempest.

Visiting an ill clansman with Tempest.

Anything but brothels and beds with Tempest.

"I'm decent," she said.

He turned around, and his jaw dropped. She was standing in a crimson gown that hugged her sinuous contours, leaving nothing to the imagination. The low-cut neckline revealed the shape of her creamy full breasts. Her nipples were hard and outlined by the thin fabric. Her raven black curls fell unbound past her waist, hugging the curves he longed to explore.

He swallowed hard. "This is going to be a very long night."

Chapter Nine

Tempest's heart had not stopped racing since they entered The Crescent Moon. Upon setting foot in the unruly establishment, she had witnessed intimacies of the flesh that she hadn't even known happened between a man and a woman.

On the one hand, she found it startling and terrifying, but, at the same time, watching the women moan softly with desire as men cupped and fondled their breasts had stirred within her a curiosity and something else—something she would have been too ashamed to admit to anyone.

But she could not lie to herself.

What she had witnessed had stirred her desire, and suddenly she was wearing a scarlet nightdress that was so sheer and feather soft that when she pulled it over her head, it had caressed her breasts and hips like a lover's touch.

And now, she was standing in front of Caleb...and they were alone.

Her face burned, and her heart raced all the more. Taking a deep breath, she raised her head and met his gaze.

His eyes bore into hers with naked desire, mirroring what blazed deep within her—hunger, wanting, needing.

"Food," he said, motioning to the bread and wine without taking his eyes off her.

She swallowed hard. "Food," she repeated.

Her heart pounded. The room smelled of musk and something that she guessed was from that deed which she had never done but wanted to do with the man who stood looking at her as if she were a tantalizing roast and he had not eaten for a week. Then suddenly, the sounds of pleasure renewed in the next room. She was so hot she thought she'd burst into flame.

"I need some fresh air," she blurted as she started toward the door.

"Absolutely not," he exclaimed, beating her there. He turned the key in the lock, then removed it, holding it tightly while he stood in front of the door like a massive barricade.

She narrowed her gaze on him. "I insist."

He crossed his arms over his chest. "Ye're not leaving this room or my side until I deliver ye into Declan's hands."

She needed to get out of there. "Then come with me."

His eyes flashed wide. "Dressed as ye are. Absolutely not! Ye look like a common whore."

Despite the truth of his words, it still stung to hear them. The heat pulsing through her combined with her desperation, creating a fury she could not contain. "Stand aside now," she hissed, clenching her fists.

He crossed his arms over his chest. "Ye'll have to go through me."

She bent her knees slightly. "Fine." Then, she charged. His eyes widened with surprise the instant before she rammed her shoulder into him.

He grunted. "Tempest, I wasn't in earnest!"

"But I was," she screeched and kicked him in the shin.

He cursed and seized her, wrapping his arms around her, but she wriggled free and caught him with an elbow in the gut.

"Ye must calm down," he urged her and lifted her off her feet.

She screamed and kicked her legs.

He lost his hold on her.

She broke free and reached for the door.

He got there first, pressing his hands against the slatted wood.

She jumped on his back.

He shook her off, but she held tightly to his tunic.

The fabric ripped.

She fell to the ground and gasped.

Layers of thin, vicious scars crisscrossed his back, covering the full expanse of his taut flesh.

He whirled around to face her but did not meet her gaze. Closing his eyes, he clenched his fists. She held her breath, not knowing what to do or say. Then his fists eased, and he calmly picked up the clean tunic, which Mary had brought him, and pulled it over his head. Then he turned to face her.

"Now ye know why I keep my tunic on."

Her mouth felt like it was stuffed with wool, and her heart pounded. The image of his back filled her mind. There must have been a thousand marks...strike after strike. "Who...who did that to ye?"

"My da," he said flatly.

She gasped, her hand covering her mouth.

"At least I think he was my da," he added.

"Ye think? Ye mean ye're not sure who whipped ye?"

He shook his head. "Nay, I know very well who did it. He did it often enough." He blew out a long breath. "'Tis complicated." Then he looked at her with concern. "Are ye all right? Did I hurt ye?"

"I'm fine," she said quickly and reached for his hand. Standing, she led him to the bed. "Tell me more," she urged him gently.

He lifted his shoulders. "There's naught to tell. I was raised by a cruel man. He kept me in shackles at night so that I couldn't run and beat me every day until the day he finally died."

"How old were ye when he died?

"Ten and four."

"Why did ye say that ye think he was yer da?"

He shook his head dismissively. "'Tis nothing."

"Tell me," she pleaded. "Please, I want to know ye."

He closed his eyes and took a deep breath. "I have few memories of my childhood not filled with him..." His words trailed off and a mirthless laugh fled his lips. "Truly, 'tis nothing but the foolish yearnings of a child."

"What? Just tell me. Don't be afraid."

He looked at her for some time. Then finally he said, "'Tis a feeling more than a memory."

"What is?"

He shrugged. "I remember..." But again his words trailed off.

"Caleb, just say it," she blurted.

He met her gaze. "I remember being loved," he said softly. "Someone loved me a long time ago. I know it." He scowled and stood abruptly. "Whenever I try to remember, all I see is his hard, twisted face." He crossed the room and stood with his back to her. "Like I said, 'tis the yearnings of a child."

She sat straighter. "Yer mother."

He turned then with a questioning look. "My mother?"

"Aye, 'tis her love that ye remember. There's nothing stronger than a mother's love."

He had a distant look in his eyes when next he spoke. "My da told me she died when I was a baby. I have no memory of her. My only true childhood memory is my own face smiling back at me." He met her gaze and shrugged. "I was my only playmate, constantly daydreaming. 'Tis how I got through each day. More than likely, I dreamt so much about being loved that it started to feel real."

Tempest's heart ached for him. She knew what it meant to have a cruel father. Her own father had been hard and unloving, but he had never struck her or her sister in anger. Not that love had stayed his hand—he had likely not thought the action worth the effort. More than anything, he had ignored his daughters. To him, she had been as insignificant as a blade of grass.

"Caleb," she rasped and crossed to his side, placing her hand on his back. Through the fabric of his tunic, she could feel the raised scars beneath her fingers. She wanted to somehow heal them, to make it all go away. Slowly, she began to lift his shirt, but he jerked away.

"Please don't," he said in a rush. "I ken 'tis...unpleasant to look upon."

She did not hesitate to reassure him. "Ye're beautiful, Caleb." The moment the words fled her lips, she felt as if she had said too much or something wrong. But she refused her fear. She would speak her truth as she always tried to do.

"So beautiful," she said again, her voice barely above a whisper.

Trembling, she reached for him—only this time he did not stop her. Slowly, tentatively, she stroked her fingertips across his skin as she circled around him. Then she splayed her hands wide on his back. He stiffened, his whole body taut like an animal about to run...or attack. Still, he did not protest. Slowly, she began to lift his shirt.

"Tempest," he breathed.

"Wheest," she whispered. She could feel him tense beneath her touch, but she didn't stop. She lifted his shirt to his shoulders, revealing his sinewy back which bore the marks of a cruel man's rage. "Ye're beautiful," she whispered again and pressed a tender kiss to his scarred flesh. His body jerked. Still, he did not pull away. She stroked her fingertips softly over the long, vicious marks, pressing her lips to his skin again and again, trying not to miss a single one as if somehow her kiss could take away all the hurt.

"Tempest," he began, his voice strained, "ye shouldn't be doing that."

She stretched her fingers wide across his back. "When will ye learn that I do what I want." Then she rested her cheek against his bare skin. "And what I want is ye."

Releasing a groan, he whirled around, crushed her close, and seized her lips in a hungry kiss. Her heart soared. she wrapped her arms around his neck and pushed her body against his. His hand raked over her curves, then grasped her bottom and lifted her feet off the ground, pressing her body against his hard length. Need pulsed through her, hot and demanding. She thrust her tongue deep inside his mouth. Their tongues danced together, hungry and wild. She dug her nails into the sinews of his brawny shoulders.

"Caleb," she cried out as all the ache, all the longing—months of pent up desire surged through her, erupting with a need she had never known.

He cupped her breast. Sensation exploded within her, searing, hot, making her feel as if her very soul could burst into flame.

"Caleb, please," she cried, moving against him.

Suddenly, he thrust her away from him.

She gasped. The loss of his touch, his heat, sent waves of cold desperation coursing through her. "Caleb," she cried, reaching for him, but he backed away. His chest heaved. His eyes burned.

"Nay," he said, taking another step back. "We cannot!"

"But why?" she demanded. "Ye can no longer deny yer feelings for me."

He closed his eyes and took a deep breath. After several moments, the tension fled his shoulders. When he opened his eyes, the fire was gone. Caleb had returned to his controlled and measured self.

"Ye're a lady," he said simply.

Her heart pounded with fury. "I don't care!"

"I know ye do not," he began calmly, "but that doesn't change who ye are, nor do yer simple tunics and unbound hair."

His words squeezed her heart in a death grip. "What I am is a woman!"

He shook his head. "Not to me."

"How...how..." Her words lodged in her throat. She turned away from him as he continued to speak.

"One day, ye will wed a nobleman, and to him ye will be a woman."

"This isn't happening," she muttered, shaking her head.

"Tempest," he said, drawing her gaze. Through her tear-filled eyes she watched him press his hand to his chest. "To me—a man without name or title—ye're a lady."

"Please, Caleb. Don't do this," she pleaded.

He drew close once more, his lips a breath from hers. His gaze full of longing. "If I could break down the barriers between us, I would." His fingers grazed her cheek. "I would pummel them to dust."

Her chest tightened. She could barely draw breath so great was the pain in her heart. She closed her eyes and cradled his hand to her cheek. "There must be a way." She opened her eyes, meeting his tender gaze, but then he took a deep breath. His hand fell away. He stepped back. The intensity of feeling vanished once again from his blue eyes. Then he bowed to her as if he were one of her tacksmen. "Ye should rest, my lady. On the morrow we will likely meet up with Declan and the rest of yer guard."

She shook her head. "Please, Caleb."

Without reply, he turned his back to her and laid down in front of the doorway and closed his eyes.

Her fury, her heartache, and sorrow collided within her. She opened her mouth. Her head fell back, but the emotion emanating from her soul did not release in a scream of anger or even a sob of agonizing regret. Nothing came out. Her loss was too great. It coiled around her soul, choking, consuming.

The man she loved did not despise her as she had once feared.

He loved her.

Caleb loved her.

She swallowed the bitter knot in her throat and stood, looking at the man who stirred her soul like no other. He lay only steps away, but he may as well have been as distant as the stars.

She remembered Alison's response when the pantler had learned of Tempest's feelings for Caleb. Alison had warned Tempest that there were conventions even she could not flout.

Tempest slumped on the edge of the bed.

Caleb was right. At birth, their fates had been decided.

Tears broke the confines of her lids. She covered her face with her hands. Her tears were not defiant or angry. They were tears of defeat, a feeling she had never known until that moment.

Caleb came to her, put his arm around her, and lifted her. Cradling her, he sat on the bed and rocked her gently, pressing soft kisses to her brow while whispering promises that everything would be all right.

But his words gave her no comfort, for how could anything be all right when the man she loved—who loved her in return—would soon bid her goodbye...forever.

Chapter Ten

Caleb awoke and looked down at the woman lying in his arms, her cheek pressed against his chest. Her silken black curls cascaded over his arm while her warm breath caressed his skin. Closing his eyes, he breathed deep her scent and wrapped his arms around her, savoring her warmth and the intimacy of their embrace.

He had faced great challenges in his life. His youth was marked by suffering. Still, he knew the hardship of his early years had made him into the man he was—resilient, controlled, exacting. He had never looked back with regret, nor had he ever longed for a different life than the one he knew; that was until he'd met Lady Tempest.

She stirred in his arms, nestling closer. The feel of her soft curves, the smell of her hair—despite their humble and garish surroundings, he felt as if he were in heaven.

But he knew the moment could not last.

Drawing a deep breath, he did the hardest thing he'd ever done. Slowly, he eased away from her sloping contours and fragrant hair. The moment he stood, he was struck by the loss of her touch. His heart ached for her. It was all he could not to pull her back into his arms and beg her to run away with him.

But he resisted.

He loved her with all that he was and all that he could ever be—and he would not allow himself to bring disgrace upon her good name.

She was not and would never be his.

"Tempest," he called softly from across the room.

She stirred. Her black lashes fluttered before opening slightly. Stretching her arm, she felt the bed beside her, then jerked upright, her brow drawn. When her gaze settled on him where he stood as far from her as he could in that small room, her features softened. A slight smile curved her lips. "Good morrow, Caleb."

He bowed to her. "My lady," he said, his voice formal.

At once, the warmth fled her eyes. Keeping her gaze downcast, she climbed out of bed, but when she raised her gaze to meet his, he took a deep breath. He recognized the fiery glint in her eyes, having witnessed its heat on many occasions. It was a look of defiance.

She raised her chin high. "I would like to break my fast in the common room."

He shook his head. "Not dressed as ye are."

She cocked her brow at him, then crossed to the wardrobe. He watched as she shifted through the items.

"This will do," she said, pulling one of Mary's tunics over the red nightdress. Then she swept her own cloak over her shoulders and tied it at her neck. Fully encased in somber black, she met his gaze with a challenging look in her eyes. "I wish to break my fast in the common room." Her chin lifted at a haughty angle. "Presently."

His nostrils flared. He knew she was baiting him by putting on the airs of her station, something he had never witnessed her do before. "Fine," he said in a clipped voice. Then he opened the door and peered into the hall. Finding it empty, he once more bowed his head. "After ye, my lady."

As regal as a queen, she strolled past him, her back straight, her chin held high. Drawing alongside her, he said in a low voice. "I ken what ye're doing."

"Whatever do ye mean?" she said innocently, her black lashes fluttering.

"Ye're demonstrating yer authority over me as a noble-woman, but remember, I've been tasked with protecting ye, even from yerself."

Her gaze flashed with anger. "I am simply being what ye've decided I am."

"Ye are what ye are," he shot back. "Neither of us have a choice."

She shook her head sadly. "I am much more than my title. If ye cannot see that, then mayhap I have given ye my affection too easily."

He wanted to seize her shoulders and vow to her that he knew her soul-deep, that he had never admired a woman more, but he understood what she refused to accept. He had no right to know her as well as he did. Making his expression impassive, he simply motioned toward the stairs. "Allow me to lead, my lady. I trust ye will be sensible and choose to return to our room if the common room is still overrun as it was last night."

"Of course," she said coolly. She reminded him of her sister, Lady Elora, when he had first met her—cold and controlling. "Now, lead the way," she continued, "as I am famished."

Again, he dipped his head to her. "As ye wish, my lady." He reached for her hand, but she snaked it away.

"'Tis not appropriate for a man, particularly a commoner like yerself, to clasp a lady's hand."

He took a deep breath, then slowly released it. "Ye're right."

He turned then and started down the stairwell, but he continued to glance back to ensure she stayed right behind him. The common room was mostly empty but for a quiet trio eating in the corner. He led Tempest to a table that had the cleanest surface. After they were seated, the barkeep came over, balancing two wooden bowls of pottage and a plate of bannock.

A smile upturned Tempest's lips as she eagerly reached for the crusty bread and inhaled its scent. "'Tis still warm!"

He smiled to himself, thinking how hard it was for her to play the unfeeling lady. She had too much passion to deny her instinctive responses.

"'Tis ye," one of the men suddenly growled from across the room.

Tempest froze just as she was about to bite into the bannock. Caleb jerked to his feet, meeting the man's gaze who was glaring at him as he stood and began to stagger toward them.

"Come no further," Caleb ordered the stranger, but he continued his drunken walk to their table.

"I saw ye," the man snarled. "I saw ye kissing my laird's betrothed."

Caleb crossed his arms over his chest. "I do not ken who ye are, but ye're clearly drunk."

The man hiccupped before pointing an unsteady finger at Caleb. "Aye, I'm drunk. I won't deny that, but 'twas ye! I swear on my father's grave, 'twas ye!"

For a moment, Caleb hesitated. Over the years, most of his dalliances with the fairer sex had been with commoners, but he had bedded both married and betrothed noblewomen whose husbands or husbands-to-be were not kind men. It was possible that Caleb had, indeed, kissed the lady in question. But at that moment, the drunk man, his laird, and his laird's betrothed were not important. Caleb jerked his head toward the stairs. "Go sleep it off."

"I will avenge my laird!" he cried, fumbling with the hilt of his sword.

Caleb groaned. "Ye leave me no choice." He pulled his fist back and caught the man under his chin. The drunkard stumbled back and collapsed on the ground. His kinsmen rushed to his side, shooting daggers at Caleb with their eyes while they dragged their fallen brother outside.

Alone but for the barkeep, Tempest met his gaze. "That was startling," she said, her tone cautious. "He seemed quite convinced that ye were at fault."

He opened his mouth, ready to assure her that to the best of his knowledge he had never broken up a happy marriage, but then, seeing the suspicion in her gaze, he hesitated. As much as it pained him, he realized, in that moment, that he needed to renew his efforts to be disagreeable—Nay, he needed to become unlovable. For how she regarded *him* did not matter at all. What mattered was that she was free to carry on and live the life for which she was destined.

Caleb waved his hand dismissively. "He's drunk. Who knows whether he was speaking of me or someone else?"

Her eyes flashed wide. "Who knows? Ye mean it could have been ye that was seen with his lady?"

He shrugged. "I've passed through this city often enough over the years. 'Tis possible he was speaking of me."

Her gaze narrowed on him. In her eyes, he could see her fury bubbling up like a pot of boiling water about to overflow. He resisted the urge to reassure her. "Anyway," he began casually, "let us eat quickly so that we can be on our way. By now, there's a chance that Declan and the others have reached the livery."

Her stony gaze held his. "Ye must be excited."

"Excited? For what reason?"

She lifted her shoulders. "Soon, ye'll be able to set out on yer own."

"Aye," he answered, his voice steady, despite the sadness that struck his heart. There was so much inside him that he wanted to tell her, but he refrained. "I'm looking forward to it," he lied.

Her eyes blazed with anger, but then her breath hitched. She looked down, letting her hair cover her face. For a moment, he thought he had pushed her too far, evoking tears rather than igniting fury. "Tempest, look at me," he urged.

"Wheest," she whispered, keeping her head downcast. "Look behind ye."

He angled his head, glancing back from the corner of his eye.

A band of men had walked into the tavern, wearing the colors of the MacKintosh.

Without hesitation, he stood and took her arm. "Keep yer head down. Do not rush."

While he led her up the stairs, he heard the unmistakable voice of Egan MacKintosh ask about any vacancies. Caleb paused on the landing and waited for the reply.

"Nay," the barkeep said. "We're full up."

"We'll pay for the whole night. Yer whores won't get a better offer."

"All my lassies are spoken for," the barkeep said firmly. "I told ye, we're full up."

"Damnation!" Egan cursed, causing Tempest to jump.

Caleb listened to the loud footfalls of the warriors leaving the tavern. When he heard the door shut, he hastened down the hall and into Mary's room, pulling Tempest behind him. Once the door closed, he spun around and met her fearful gaze.

"I saw him," she said in a rush. "I saw Egan."

Caleb raked his hand through his hair. "I ken."

"Do ye think he followed us? Do ye think he knows that we're here?"

Caleb shook his head. "He would have forced his way upstairs to search the rooms." He reached for his saddlebags. "Like us, he is simply trying to find accommodations; however, I do believe he came to Inverness in search of ye."

Her eyes widened still. "This is bad."

He nodded. "It isn't good, that's for certain." Slinging his saddlebags over his shoulders, he was about to tell her to gather her things, but then he realized that she may be safer in The Crescent Moon, than any place else. More than that, he saw an opportunity to truly earn her anger.

Clearing his throat, he reached for the door. "I'm going to the stables to see if Declan and the others have arrived."

She grabbed his arm. "But what about me?"

"Ye must stay here," he said firmly.

"But ye said that ye wouldn't leave my side, not until ye handed me over to Declan's care."

He gave her a pointed look. "That was before the wharf became teeming with MacKintosh warriors."

She lifted her head high. "Ye cannot leave me here. I can fight. Give me a sword!"

He shook his head. "Ye're a force to be reckoned with, Tempest. This I do not doubt, nor do I doubt that I will pay dearly for what I am about to do."

Ignoring her cries of protest, he scooped her into his arms and tossed her on the straw mattress before he quickly threw open the door and shut it behind him. Withdrawing the key from his sporran, he locked the door the instant before she started to pound on it.

"Caleb," she yelled. "Caleb!"

Her screeching demands followed him down the hallway, shooting through him like arrows straight to his heart. He stopped in his tracks, wanting to turn back and never leave her side again.

But that was not his place.

It pained him to leave her locked in a small room. She was not meant to be confined. She was meant to be free, racing over the moors, her beautiful hair unbound, her face beaming with joy.

Still, he forced one foot in front of the other, telling himself that he was doing the right thing. In fact, knowing Tempest as well as he did, imprisoning her—even for her own safety—was likely an unforgiveable offense, which meant he was well on his way to accomplishing the goal of ensuring she fell out of love with him. Now, all he had to do was commit a few more unforgiveable misdeeds, and she would cast him aside.

Sorrow clutched his heart.

Meanwhile, he would love her until his dying day.

Chapter Eleven

Tempest banged her fists again and again on the door. "Caleb! Don't do this! Come back!"

She stopped and pressed her ear to the slatted wood, hearing the now familiar sounds of the brothel—peels of raucous laughter and men speaking loudly. Holding her breath, she strained to hear any footfalls over the sound of a nearby headboard knocking against the wall.

"Caleb!" she shouted again and resumed her banging. She kept pounding until her fists throbbed. Tears stung her eyes. Breathing heavily, she rested her forehead against the door and flexed her aching fingers.

"Damn ye, Caleb," she breathed out in defeat and slumped on the bed, cradling her head in her hands.

How could he have left her behind?

She knew that he believed he was making the safe choice, that he was protecting her and fulfilling his promise to Nathan and Elora, but as usual he was being too damn cautious. Meanwhile, she did not doubt that they could have outwitted Egan and his men.

Together, nothing could stand in their way, including conventions like titles and birthrights. But he never listened to his heart and certainly paid no heed to her own.

She squeezed her fists, feeling as if a storm brewed within her, straining the confines of her body.

She needed Storm. She needed to take to the open moors and ride before everything inside her shattered.

"I have to get out of here," she cried, rushing at the door. Again, she pounded with all her might. "Please, Caleb!"

Pain shot up her arms. She collapsed to her knees. "But he loves me," she whispered. Leaning against the door, she fought to catch her breath. Slowly, her arms and legs went numb, and then that was all that was left.

No feeling.

Only emptiness.

She remained in a daze for some time, when suddenly a soft rapping sounded against the wall, coming from the adjacent room. She straightened and winced when she stood. Forcing her feet to walk toward the noise, she crossed the room and pressed her ear to the wall. She was about to ask who was on the other side, but she hesitated, fearful that Egan might have returned and set a trap for her.

"'Tis Mary," a woman's voice called softly.

Relieved, Tempest felt her legs strengthen. "Mary, I'm here."

Mary chuckled. "I know that. I've been listening to yer attempts to break down my door for some time." Then she cleared her throat. "I don't wish to intrude, but I thought ye might need some company."

Tempest perked up. "But how? I'm locked inside. Do ye have another key?"

"Nay," Mary answered.

Tempest hung her head, releasing a heavy breath. She would have no choice but to wait until Caleb's return. But then she was struck by a fresh terror. What if Caleb encountered Egan and his men on his way to find Declan?

"Mary, ye have to get me out of here!"

Suddenly, the tapestry next to her moved, then lifted away from the wall and Mary's face peered out from behind it.

"If that is yer wish," she said with a wink. Then she came fully into the room and dipped in a low curtsy. "My lady."

Tempest stiffened with surprise. "How did ye know I was a lady?"

Mary smiled and tossed her long red hair over her shoulder. Her skin was scrubbed clean. She was as beautiful and welcome as the sun on a summer's day. "I had my suspicions when I met ye." She raised her brow slightly, giving Tempest a knowing look. "'Tis in yer bearing, in the way ye walk and how ye speak."

Tempest couldn't help the smile that upturned her lips. "If only Firtha could hear ye now."

Mary's brow crinkled. "Who?"

"Never mind," Tempest said quickly. "'Tis not important. Go on."

A cunning smile lit Mary's face. "The walls are thin." She lifted her shoulders with a shrug. "Bridget and I could not help but overhear yer...er...discussions with yer handsome guard."

Tempest blushed. "Ye heard everything?"

Mary nodded. "Everything. And I don't mind telling ye that we couldn't help but listen. We were too enthralled by yer love story."

Tempest's stomach sank. "Our story is over before it's begun."

Mary cocked a brow at her. "Hardly"

"Ye weren't listening closely enough. There is no happy ending, not for us. Whether this day or the next, we will soon part ways, and I will never see him again."

Mary put her hands on her hips. "Ye don't strike me as the type of lass who gives up so easily."

Tempest shot her a defensive look. "Were ye listening at all? Our love is forbidden."

Mary began to fan herself with her hand as if she were suddenly warm. "There's nothing more appealing than forbidden love. This I know as I've had my share of noblemen. But in yer case, Bridget and I believe that ye truly do love each other."

"What difference does that make?"

Mary looked shocked by Tempest's question. "'Tis everything. 'Tis the only thing that matters. Ye must fight for him!"

"How can I, when he has refused me?"

"He hasn't refused ye," Mary began, "He's only trying to protect ye. But ye're the noblewoman. Ye're the one who must make the grand gesture."

"What do ye mean?"

"Ye must make the sacrifice either by relinquishing yer title or demanding yer father agree to the match."

"My father is dead," Tempest replied. "'Tis my sister and her new husband who will determine my fate."

Mary released a heavy sigh. "Then ye're sister must be terribly unkind."

"Nay," Tempest said, quick to defend Elora. "My sister is loving and generous."

"Truly? Then ye must fear that her new husband will refuse the match."

Tempest shook her head. "Actually, Caleb is his closest friend."

Mary threw her arms up. "Then what are ye going on about? Why don't ye simply press yer sister for her blessing?"

"'Tis not as easy as that. Caleb brings nothing to my clan by way of fortune or alliance. He would never allow it."

Mary pressed her hand to her heart. "He's so thoughtful, putting the good of the clan first. So then, yer coffers must need filling."

Tempest straightened. "Nay, Clan Brodie's coffers and stores are full."

A smile suddenly brightened Mary's face. "That is a splendid thing." But then, her smiled faded. "He must worry over the safety of yer borders."

"Well, we do have one neighbor who gives us a great deal of trouble, but Clan Brodie has stronger alliances with our other neighbors."

To Tempest's surprise Mary started to laugh.

"How can ye be laughing at a time such as this?" Tempest demanded.

Mary shook her head and sighed. Then she took Tempest's hands and gave her a gentle smile. "In case ye didn't notice, we've run out of reasons for why ye cannot fight for the man ye love."

Tempest considered Mary's words. Then she looked Mary hard in the eye. "Ye're right, aren't ye?"

Mary simply nodded.

Tempest stood up and started to pace. "I am the lady. Even if he should try to stop me, I still will ask my sister for permission." She paused mid-step. "In fact, I can order him to remain by my side. Should he try to leave, I will forbid him."

A glint lit Mary's eyes. "Aye, forbid him, my lady. No man can resist what they're told they cannot have."

Tempest tossed her hair off her shoulder and started toward the door, but then she faltered, hearing Firtha and Murray gasp in her mind. "I must get to the livery near the cathedral." She gave Mary a hopeful smile. "But I shouldn't go alone. Will ye come with me?"

Mary smiled. "Of course."

At that moment, Tempest remembered the reason why Caleb had locked her away to begin with. "That neighbor of which I spoke who gives us trouble from time to time, well, he is actually here, in Inverness. Earlier, he was in this very tavern. Before ye agree to join me, ye should know the risks. Ye see, *I* am what he covets most."

Mary's eyes flashed wide. "What do ye mean?"

"I mean he wishes to marry me. If given the chance, he'll likely abduct me and find the first priest willing to overlook my protests for a fee."

Mary shrugged. "We'll just have to be careful then, won't we? Now, my lady, are ye ready to fight for the man ye love?"

Tempest stood straight and set her hands on her hips. "I've never surrendered a day in my life. I'm certainly not going to start now. What does it matter if *he* is not willing to break social ranks—I am! And I believe that my sister and my people will support me. Caleb is worth ten noblemen."

Mary opened her mouth as if to speak, but then she shook her head and started to fuss with Tempest's cloak. "This fabric is too fine," she muttered. "My tunic is suitable. Ye'll have to keep yer hood drawn."

Tempest searched Mary's face. "What were ye going to tell me just now?"

"'Tis nothing," Mary replied.

"Please," Tempest urged. "If we are going to do this, we must be honest with one another."

Mary did not reply straightaway. Tempest chewed her lip, trying to remain patient.

Finally, Mary nodded. "Ye're right." She squeezed Tempest's hand. "Forgive my boldness, my lady, but judging from what I overheard when ye and Caleb were...er...*talking*, yer sister is not the only one who may need convincing of Caleb's worth."

Brows drawn, Tempest asked, "What do ye mean?"

Mary shrugged. "I've known a lot of men. They may seem as strong as castle walls on the outside, but inside...well, they have their doubts and worries."

Tempest remembered how ashamed Caleb was of his scars. To him, they were 'unpleasant to look upon'—while, to Tempest, there was nothing that could diminish his appeal. Still, she realized that Mary was right. Caleb's scars ran deeper than the flesh. She did not doubt that the abuse he had suffered in his youth cut straight to his soul.

But she was determined to save his soul.

"I am going to fight for him," Tempest said, steeling her shoulders. "Even if that means fighting him."

Mary gave her an approving look. "I believe ye're ready now."

"Nothing can stop me," Tempest declared. She turned and crossed the room to the door. Grasping the handle, she said, "I will not rest until Caleb is mine!" She yanked on the latch, but the door did not budge. Laughter bubbled up her throat as she turned back to Mary. "'Tis still locked."

Mary smiled in return. "I would have said something, but I wanted ye to have yer moment." She lifted the tapestry. "Follow me. We still have to finish dressing and visit the kitchen."

Tempest followed Mary into the next room. Straightaway, her gaze settled on the woman sitting up in bed. Her soft brown hair was woven into a thick plait and was so long that it coiled in a puddle beside her on the sheet. She had bright green eyes, set deeply in her heart-shaped face. Tempest dipped in a curtsy. "Ye must be Bridget."

Bridget smiled, revealing a space between her front teeth that lent her otherwise flawless features a hint of mischief and sensual appeal. She folded her hands on her round stomach. "Good morrow, my lady. Welcome."

Tempest smiled. "Thank ye and thank ye for lending me yer nightdress."

"She'll be needing to borrow yer cloak now, too, Brig," Mary said, chiming in.

Tempest shot Mary a questioning look. "But my cloak is dry."

"And too fine by far to walk the streets as a commoner."

Mary's gaze trailed over Tempest, while she scrutinized her appearance. "Ye must wear that fancy piece that goes over the lot."

"But my surcote will not help me look more common."

A savvy glimmer shone in Mary's eye. "We want to play our hand right and keep that card hidden beneath the cloak. With ye having trouble with a laird, being able to reveal yerself as a lady may welcome aid otherwise denied to us. But hopefully, we will just be three commoners making our way through the city to enjoy the festivities."

"Three commoners?" Tempest said. "Who is to join us?"

"I'm quite certain that a lady and her maid wouldn't walk the streets of Inverness alone," Mary said with a wink. "There's a strong lad, who works in the kitchen, named Henry. He looks older than ten and four. He'll pass as a guard just in case ye do need to suddenly become Lady Tempest."

In that moment, Tempest realized how fortunate it was that there had been no other rooms available in the city. "Ye've thought of everything," she beamed.

Mary blushed at her praise. "I don't know about that, my lady." She cleared her throat. "Now, let's get ye ready."

~ * ~

When Tempest finally stepped out onto the dirt road in front of the tavern flanked by Mary and the kitchen lad, Henry, she took a deep breath, enjoying the rush of freedom. "Shall we?" she said to her companions before starting off in what she was sure was the direction of the city center.

"Not that way," Henry said quickly. Then he stopped, and a blush tinted his cheeks. "My lady," he said, which made his cheeks burn a brighter red. Tempest smiled at the young lad who was clearly a little tongue-tide by her presence.

"What did I tell ye, Henry?" Mary snapped. "At least for now, she's as common as one of us."

Tempest glanced down, ensuring her surcote was fully hidden beneath her borrowed and humble-looking cloak. Then she met Henry's gaze. "I prefer to be called Tempest anyway."

Although she never would have thought it possible, Henry's cheeks burned brighter still. It was hard to remember that he was only ten and four with his great height and broad shoulders. But if ye looked closely, ye could see his youth in his flaxen hair, the rounded apples of his cheeks, and dancing eyes. He was the sort of lad that she could picture still taking pleasure in chasing a butterfly through the Heather, at least when no one else was looking.

He stood tall, thrusting his chest out, trying very hard to appear like a lady's guard. "There is a shorter way and one less traveled," he said.

Tempest smiled. "Lead on then, Henry."

He started to bow awkwardly, but then froze and cleared his throat before turning on his heel and leading them down a narrow alley.

"Henry has never met a lady before," Mary explained quietly. "Ye've got him all flustered."

"Even if I wasn't trying to look the part of a commoner. He needn't stand on formality for me." She tugged at the surcote beneath her cloak, which Mary had tied as tightly as Firtha might. "In fact, I find the conventions stifling to the spirit." She took the deepest breath that her bindings would allow and scanned the road ahead for the bright reds and greens of the MacKintosh plaid. "I just hope we can avoid meeting Egan. He has a cruel heart. I do not wish any harm to befall ye or Henry."

Mary squeezed her hand. "Ye needn't worry about us. Dealing with unsavories as I call that type is something to which we're accustomed. I'm not afraid of men like that. Cowards the lot of them."

"Ye're right about that. Egan is a coward." Tempest considered the woman walking beside her. "Thank ye, Mary. For all ye've done for me."

Mary smiled at her and gave a quick shrug with her shoulders. "I can't resist a good love story." A distant look came into her eyes. "Makes me think there's hope for us all."

Now it was Tempest's turn to squeeze Mary's hand. "After I convince Caleb that he's worthy of love and to accept my hand in marriage, I'll ask him if he has any eligible friends."

Mary burst out laughing. "Now, I'm even more determined to help ye win yer man."

Spurred on by Mary's enthusiasm, Tempest pulled her into a faster gait. "Let us hurry! We're bound to find Caleb at the stables, and surely by now the captain of my guard and the rest of my men will be there as well."

Tempest's thoughts turned to Declan. She did not doubt his regard for Caleb. Surely, she would be able to convince him that she and Caleb were destined for each other.

They reached the end of the alley and stepped out onto a busy cobbled road that opened to a large, crowded courtyard, filled with vendors. Scanning the revelers, she expelled a long breath. Before she could convince Caleb to follow his heart and Declan that she should be able to marry for love, she had to find them. More than that, she had to make certain that Egan did not find her first.

They made it to the other side of the courtyard. Then she followed Henry through a maze of narrow alleyways. All the while, she continued to scan their surroundings, searching for her clan's colors, and at the same time, remaining alert to the presence of her enemy. Still, as much as she tried to remain focused on their path, there was a nagging voice inside her head that made her heart tighten in her chest.

Once again, she had allowed herself to hope.

Not just to hope—she was pursuing a man who from his own lips had told her they could have no future together.

She shook her head, refusing the doubt building in her mind.

This time was different.

This time, she did not doubt Caleb's feelings for her as she had done in the past.

Now, she simply had to show him that they had a right be together. After all, there could be no greater gift from the Heavens. Even the scriptures say that God is love. To deny what was in their hearts would be to put the will of man before the will of God.

And she had never surrendered her will to any man.

But Caleb was not like her.

He wasn't reckless. In fact, he was downright cautious. More than that, he was a man without a name, and this might be what would tear them apart for all time.

"He can be such an idiot," she said aloud.

"Henry is doing the best he can," Mary said quickly. "We cannot go any faster. There are too many people."

Tempest shook her head. "Ye misunderstand me. I would never speak ill of Henry." She sighed. "I was just thinking out loud. Please, believe me when I say that Henry is everything a guide should be and more."

A knowing look settled on Mary's features. "Ye were thinking about Caleb."

Tempest nodded. "I was. I'm worried that his stubborn nature will be our undoing."

"From my experience men are often idiots, but never underestimate the power of persistence."

Tempest pushed her shoulders back. "Ye're right. 'Tis merely a battle of wills, which is one battle I know I can win."

Mary shifted her gaze forward. "Ready yer armor then," she said as they stepped into an expansive courtyard packed with people. On one side, Inverness Cathedral stood watch over the square with its imposing north and south facing towers. At the center of the square, rising above the heads of those who gathered, was a statue of Saint Andrew, and to the left Tempest spied the livery.

"So many people," she exclaimed, wondering how they would ever find Caleb or Declan in such a thick crowd.

"Many of these people are pilgrims waiting to pray to Saint Columba," Henry began, "soon the bells will ring for Mass. Our search will be easier then."

Tempest nodded as she tried to scan the bustling yard. "We will also have to be more cautious. When this crowd thins out, I will be easier to spot by a MacKintosh warrior."

"Pull yer hood down lower," Henry suggested.

Tempest did as he had bidden. Then she looked to the stables. "Let's start there. 'Tis where Declan said he would meet us. Surely, this is where Caleb would have gone first."

As they picked their way toward the stable entrance, Tempest's stomach fluttered with nerves. What if Caleb held stubbornly to what he believed was right? He was just that sort of man—the kind that would make the ultimate sacrifice for love.

"Have faith," she told herself and stepped inside the livery.

It felt like coming home.

The air was hot and smelled of horses and hay. She blew out a slow, steady breath, allowing the familiar surroundings to calm her nerves. Scanning the long building, she took in the sturdy stalls and the variety of horses. Stable-hands and numerous travelers milled about. The clomping of hooves mingled with the choir of voices and snorting beasts.

"Do ye see any of yer men?" Mary asked.

Tempest shook her head. "Not yet."

Just then the rich sound of the chapel bell rang out, calling to the pilgrims. And before too long, the livery was empty, or at least it had appeared that way.

"Do ye hear that?" Mary said, a mischievous expression shaping her features.

Tempest paused and listened. Intruding upon the familiar sounds of the stables was a soft, rhythmic noise. Tempest shrugged. "'Tis one of the horses."

Mary cocked a brow at her. "Ye really are a virgin, aren't ye?"

"I don't see what that has to—"

"Wheest," Mary said with a grin. "Come on."

Tempest followed her new friend while Henry trailed behind. The noise became louder and louder. Tempest could feel her cheeks burn as she realized the sound matched the steady knocking of headboards against the walls of The Crescent Moon.

With a soft giggle, Mary pointed to one of the stalls. "They're in there," she said. Then she crossed to the gate and peeked between the slats. A moment later, she motioned for Tempest to look.

Tempest shook her head.

But Mary pulled her close. "Aren't ye even the littlest bit curious?"

Tempest took a deep breath.

Of course she was curious.

"Fine," Tempest said and took up Mary's spot. Closing one eye, she pressed her face close to peer between the gap in the slats. She glimpsed a woman, sitting astride a man whose legs were visible beneath her bunched skirts. His hands gripped her waist. She was riding him like a horse. Despite her burning cheeks, Tempest could not look away, although she knew she should. But the sight stirred something within her. She imagined herself as the woman, and Caleb beneath her.

How she wanted to be like them. She craved it with her whole being.

Just then the man's hands seized the woman's waist and plucked her off his lap. Tempest gasped at the sight of his bare, hard member. Then her gaze shifted to his face.

Her breath caught. She stumbled back.

Mary grabbed her arm. "Tempest!"

Tempest couldn't breathe. Her whole body shook. "Nay," she said out loud. Her head felt like it was on fire. "Nay," she cried louder.

Mary rushed back to the stall and peered inside. An instant later, she banged on the gate and shouted, "Ye bastard!"

The pounding of Mary's fist echoed in Tempest's mind.

Henry grasped her arm. "Come, my lady!"

Tempest jerked her arm free. The world was spinning. Her stomach twisted. A knot rose in her throat. Tears blurred her eyes. She turned on her heel and ran from the stables. Covering her face with her hands, she did not slow down.

"How could he?" she sobbed.

And then she struck something hard.

Fingers bit into her arms.

Her hands fell away from her face, and she opened her eyes. She had run straight into Laird Egan MacIntosh.

"Nay," she raged, pushing at his hard, barrel chest.

"Ye couldn't wait to feel my arms around ye, eh?" Egan jeered.

He leaned close. His sour breath assailed her nostrils. "Get away from me!" Her knee shot up, connecting with his groin. He cried out and released her. She shot forward, but then fell back as he yanked on her cloak. The fabric ripped. She strained to hold her footing but lost her balance and fell back, hard. The wind knocked out of her. She fought for breath. Egan seized her, grabbing her arms. He picked her off the ground.

"Ye will pay for that, wife," he snarled.

Fear and anger surged through her. Her lungs opened. She sucked in a breath. "I'm not yer wife!"

"Not yet," Egan said, his face twisting in a wicked grin.

A storm, emanating from her soul, erupted inside her. With all her strength and all her fury, she fought Egan's hold. Losing herself to the wildness within, she screamed her rage, lashing out with her fists and legs. He pinned her arms and covered her mouth with his hand, but she clamped down hard, biting with all her might. Again, he cried out and threw her to the ground.

"I will beat ye to submission," he shouted, his voice like thunder.

He grabbed her surcote and lifted her once again in the air. His face shone red with fury. He pulled his hand back to strike her. She closed her eyes and tensed against the threat of pain.

But it was Egan who cried out.

Once again, she fell to the ground. She looked up and gasped.

Caleb was holding Egan's arm, twisting it behind her enemy's back.

"That is no way to treat a lady," Caleb snarled.

"This is none of yer affair," Egan spat, straining to escape Caleb's hold. Caleb released him, then stepped in front of her, shielding her from the laird's menacing gaze.

"She is mine, promised to me," Egan snarled.

Tempest stepped around Caleb. "That's a lie, and ye know it," she shouted at Egan.

Caleb's arm flashed out, blocking her from going too close to the enemy.

"Ye're sister broke our betrothal," Egan sneered. "'Tis only fitting that ye replace the prize I've lost."

"We have no contract," Tempest snapped. "'Tis fitting that ye leave me alone."

Caleb stepped closer to Egan, his stance strong. "She clearly wants nothing to do with ye. Back down and be on yer way."

"This is none of yer affair," Egan growled again.

"I decide what is and what is not my affair," Caleb said. A warning entered his voice as he continued, "now stand aside or else I'll be forced to ruin the festivities for ye and yer men."

Egan glanced around the courtyard. Tempest did the same, spying her friends. Mary, her brow drawn with worry, was standing near the stables with a tight grip on Henry's arm, keeping him from entering the fray. There also were a few stablehands who had stopped working to watch the confrontation, but otherwise everyone else had gone to Mass.

Freed from Egan's grasp, Tempest started toward where Mary and Henry were standing, but two MacKintosh warriors stepped in front of her blocking her way.

"Please Declan," she murmured under her breath. She prayed for her captain and the rest of the Brodie warriors to suddenly ride into the courtyard, swords raised at the ready.

They would teach Egan a lesson.

She shifted her gaze back to Caleb who stood staring menacingly at Egan.

She crossed her arms over her chest. Then *she* would teach Caleb a lesson.

"Ye're alone and unarmed," Egan scoffed at Caleb, raising his fist in the air.

But Caleb held up his hand. "Before ye signal to yer men, know this—I always fight to the death."

"Then I look forward to watching ye die," Egan taunted before he snapped his fist down.

"Look out," Tempest cried as one of Egan's warriors charged at Caleb, holding his sword a loft.

Caleb stood his ground, then dropped low, whirling in a circle with his leg extended, catching his attacker mid-stride. The warrior shot forward, crashed to the ground, and drop his sword. Caleb seized the fallen warrior's blade, jumped to his feet, and turned to face the rest of the MacKintosh warriors. "Come and get me," he snarled, his face twisted with a fury that stole Tempest's breath. It was as if he was suddenly possessed by the devil himself.

Tempest gasped as half a dozen MacIntosh warriors sounded their battle cries and raced at Caleb, all with swords raised at the ready.

Caleb parried the first blow, then struck. His sword sliced through the warrior's belly.

A scream fled Tempest's lips. An instant later, Caleb used his foot to free his sword from the dying man's body, only to turn and run another warrior through. She couldn't believe her eyes. With vicious and merciless fury, Caleb parried and struck again and again, his blade dripping red with blood. Men littered the ground. He jumped over a body and charged at Egan.

"Nay!" she shrieked.

The laird's face twisted with vengeful fury, but his skill was no match for Caleb's. Egan dropped his sword and ran. But before Tempest knew what was happening, Caleb threw his blade. The silver glinted in the sun before it sank into Egan's back. The laird's mouth opened, but no sound came out. Then he fell to the ground. Dead.

She covered her mouth with her hand. Her heart pounded. She looked at Caleb whose face was hard and cold. She tried to speak, but words would not come. Her gaze scanned the fallen men. So much blood. So much death.

"How...how..." She sputtered. Bile rose in her throat. "How could ye do that?"

The hardness left Caleb's face. He shrugged his shoulders and cocked a brow at her. "I did what I had to."

"Ye killed Egan in cold blood! Ye already had me. Ye could have just taken me." Her stomach twisted. "What are we going to do?" Her mind was spinning. She scanned the faces of the MacIntosh warriors. Her gaze met blank stares. She fought to breathe. "Dear God above!"

"Having just rescued ye, I thought ye'd be more grateful," Caleb said, drawing her gaze.

Tears fought for release, but it was her fury that took hold of her. "Grateful," she cried, lunging at him. She pummeled his chest with her fist. "Ye've started a war!"

"I saved yer life," he replied. "Ye would do well to remember that." Before she knew what was happening, he seized her and threw her over his shoulder.

"Put me down!" she shouted. "Ye'll pay for this when Declan arrives!"

A heartbeat later, Mary and Henry raced at Caleb. "Put her down ye beast!" Mary shouted.

Caleb stopped. "Get back," he snapped at her would-be rescuers, shoving Henry to the ground.

Tempest knew that Mary and Henry had no choice but to heed his words, lest they meet the same end as the dead warriors now littering Cathedral Square.

Confusion, fury, and heartache collided inside her. The sound that tore from her lips was akin to that made by a wild animal as she strained to break free from his hold. She kicked and struck his back with her fists.

But he didn't flinch.

"How could ye?" she shouted again. "And the woman in the stables...how could ye?"

He made no reply, no denials or pleas to be forgiven.

Her heart shattered. Pain like she had never known consumed her. Ceasing her struggle, she hung limp over his shoulder, surrendering to the knowledge that she had, indeed, misjudged him.

The cobbled and dirt ground sped beneath her blurred gaze. Before too long, she was carried into a building, the nature of which she could not see, but judging by the sounds, it might have been the common room of an inn or tavern. Then she grunted, bouncing on his shoulder as he jogged up a staircase. His footfalls pounded across a long hallway. She heard the click of a key in a lock before a door swung wide, and he unceremoniously tossed her on a thin feather-tick mattress. The breath knocked out of her.

Gasping for air, she met Caleb's gaze as she struggled to fill her lungs. He looked at her, his face hard and unreadable. Then he dipped his head. "My lady." He smiled, something that would normally make her knees weak, but this time all she wanted to do was punch it off his face. Still, she couldn't breathe. The string of curses and insults remained lodged in her restricted throat.

Turning, he walked back out into the hallway. The door shut just as air rushed back into her lungs.

"Nay," she cried out. Rushing to the doorway, she raised her fist to pound the slatted wood, but her body sagged. Her knees gave way. She slid to the floor. Resting her head in her arms, she let her tears fall.

Once again, Caleb had locked her in a room.

Chapter Twelve

The sun shone high in the sky when Declan, Nachlan, and the rest of the Brodie warriors rode into Inverness. Market stalls had been erected beyond the confines of the numerous squares as every merchant, peddler, and tradesman sought to pad their purses with the arrival of so many pilgrims and travelers to town. Maneuvering through the cramped streets on horseback required patience that Declan simply did not have at that moment.

"Move along," he shouted at people gathering to visit together in the middle of the road. Nudging his horse forward when they dispersed, he scanned the busy roadsides and divergent alleyways, searching for the colors of Clan Brodie and Clan MacKintosh, but all the while, he longed to gallop to the livery where Caleb and Lady Tempest awaited their arrival...or so he prayed.

His chest tightened against the foreboding in his heart. The protection of Lady Tempest was his responsibility. He had hated to leave her to another's care, even Caleb's. Over the last several months, Declan had spent a great deal of time in Caleb's company and had grown to respect his new laird's closest friend. Still, Declan could not help but worry. He did not doubt that Caleb would do his best to safeguard her; however, Declan knew more than most that Lady Tempest's reckless spirit had a way of finding trouble.

Declan clenched his jaw as his concern mounted with every passing moment.

"Blast," he muttered under his breath when they had to bring their horses to a halt to allow a procession of pilgrims to pass.

Declan had already been on edge, but recent events had added to his worry.

When they'd arrived the evening before at Frasier territory, he accepted the chieftain's hospitality and dined at the high dais in the great hall, even though he hadn't the stomach for it. Following the evening meal, they'd been given leave to retire early, for which Declan was grateful. While the rest of his men had rolled out their pallets beside the hearth in the great hall, he'd been given a room in the keep.

But now he wished he had refused Laird Frasier's gesture of hospitality and instead bedded down with his men.

Mayhap then his heart would not be pounding as hard as it was.

He knew that it may have been a dream or one of the kitchen lads making mischief. Still, a chill raked up Declan's spine when he once again remembered what had occurred earlier that morrow before the cock crowed...

Declan was lying on the bed, awaiting first light to rouse his men, when he heard a knock at his door.

But not just any knock.

He heard the pounding knock of three.

His breath hitched. He lunged out of bed and threw open the door.

No one was there.

He stumbled back, his heart racing.

In his mind, flashed memories of his ol' gran. He could still hear her scratchy voice warning him..."Remember, my lad, when ye hear the pounding knock of three and no one is at the door, it means that someone is going to die."

"Nay," Declan blurted out loud.

"What is it?" Nachlan said, turning to meet his gaze.

"'Tis nothing," Declan replied quickly. But no matter how he tried, he couldn't shake the memory, and too much misfortune had occurred since they set out from Castle Bron for him to shrug off the ill omen.

He glanced over at Nachlan, wishing to unburden his soul and tell his clansmen about what had happened. But he wasn't certain if the younger man kept faith in omens nor did he want to distract his best warrior.

Shaking his head to regain his focus, Declan tightened his grip on the reins. "Keep sharp, lads," he called to his men. "Let's find our lady!"

When at last, they came upon Cathedral Square, Declan was surprised to see that the crowd was at its thickest yet. But there was no song or gaiety, nor was there the solemnity of pilgrims waiting for the Cathedral bell to call for *Vespers*.

People were whispering, making the sign of the cross and shaking their heads grimly.

"What do ye make of that?" Declan asked Nachlan, pointing to the center of the square where the people had formed a circle. Many were pushing through to see what was happening only to retreat an instant later.

Nachlan shook his head. "My view is no better than yers."

"Right." Declan dismounted. "Ye come with me," he said to Nachlan. Then he handed his reins to the nearest Brodie guard. "The rest of ye, remain here with the horses but watch for my signal should I need ye."

Declan turned back to the throng in front of him and squared his shoulders. Then he began to push his way through. When he cleared the front line of people and stepped into the open, he gasped and stumbled back, and in his head blasted the pounding knock of three.

Someone, indeed, had died.

There, on the ground, his eyes staring vacantly at the heavens above, was Egan, Laird of Clan MacKintosh. Declan's heart pounded. His gaze fell on another slain MacKintosh warrior and then another. More than half a dozen men lay on the ground, blood pooling around their lifeless bodies.

"Dear God above," Nachlan muttered, his voice weak.

Declan shook his head as stunned as his kinsmen. He didn't know what to say or do. Then, just opposite him, a young lad pushed through the crowd to view the scene, but he was jostled by someone behind him and fell, nearly landing on one of the bodies.

Declan's head cleared, and he stepped forward. "Get back," he shouted. His gaze scanning the rows of onlookers. "Give them their dignity!"

Some people began to back away. Declan waved over his head to his men who started to clear the area, using their horses to force people back.

"Check the stables for our lady," Declan ordered Nachlan before he knelt at Laird MacKintosh's side. First making the sign of the cross, Declan unclasped the top fold of Egan's plaid and turned it into a shroud to cover the dead man's face.

"She isn't there," Nachlan said when he returned. "But ye must come with me!"

"Cover the rest of them," Declan told his men. Then he followed Nachlan to the steps of the cathedral where a man clad in the MacKintosh plaid sat while a nun tended his wounds. Dried blood streaked the side of his face and neck and oozed from the linen bandage surrounding his head.

When Declan approached, the man looked up. His forlorn expression bloomed with vengeful life. He tried to stand but was clearly too weak. He fell back on the steps and settled for pointing his uninjured arm at Declan. "Murderer," the man cried, his angry eyes boring into Declan's.

Declan held his hands up, refusing blame. "I've only just arrived in the city."

"'Tis all yer clan's doing," the man snarled.

"Enough," a priest cried as he rushed out onto the cathedral steps. "Do not cast yer aspersions here at the house of God!"

Declan knelt on one knee and bowed his head. "I only seek answers for the blood spilled this day." Standing, he motioned to where the bodies lay, shrouded in their own plaids. "I know those men. Their clan neighbors mine to the north."

"His kinsman stabbed my laird in the back," the wounded man spat. He slumped on the stairs, breathing hard.

The priest eyed Declan with suspicion. "Is yer kinsman responsible?"

Declan shook his head. "Nay, Father. My men and I have only just arrived in the city. The only Brodie of our clan in Inverness has been our lady and her guard. He is not my kin by birth but has earned his place among us."

The priest's gaze narrowed. "Does yer lady have black hair and a fierce spirit?"

Declan's shoulders tensed. There was no good reason why the priest would know Lady Tempest so well. "Aye," Declan admitted. "How, may I ask, could ye have such knowledge of her?"

The priest descended several steps while he kept his gaze fixed on Declan. "I witnessed the desecration of our holy square."

The wounded man sat up again. "None of this would have happened if yer lady had honored my laird's rightful claim!"

Declan's voice remained steady. "Yer laird never had right to the hand of either Brodie lady." Declan shifted his gaze to meet the priest's. "There was discussion about a betrothal between the eldest lady and Laird MacKintosh, but it was never made official. Her father died before a contract was signed." Declan gestured to the injured man. "This man's laird has since pursued the younger sister's hand, who ye just described, but out of vengeance and spite, without contract or blessing. In life, he lacked honor…" Declan paused and pressed his lips together for a moment before continuing, "I will say no more as it is unholy to speak of the dead."

The priest took another step down and now stood eye to eye with Declan. "I saw yer lady, and Laird MacKintosh did, indeed, accost her."

Declan felt a rush of anger, knowing Lady Tempest had been in peril, but then he remembered that Egan and his men were now dead. "But what happened? How did they meet their death?"

"I told ye," the wounded man spat. "'Twas yer man!"

Brows drawn, Declan turned back to the priest in confusion.

"A tall, dark-haired man of moderate build rushed to her aid. For a moment, I was relieved by his presence, but then the fighting ensued." The priest's voice dropped as if he did not wish the saints or angels to hear his words. "Yer man unleashed his fury upon their souls." The priest's voice grew even softer as he continued, "he did as this man said. His laird tried to run, but yer man cut him down, stabbing him in the back. I've never witnessed anything so shamelessly savage."

"Forgive me, Father, but ye must be mistaken. Caleb is a steady man of good character. He's not given over to violence unless he had no other choice."

"Caleb did ye call him?" the priest asked.

Declan nodded. "Aye, that is his name."

"What is his family name?"

"I do not ken," Declan admitted.

The priest raised his brow. "What is his trade?"

Declan cleared his throat. "He's...er...he's a bounty hunter."

The priest shook his head in disapproval. "Such men are not known to be peacemakers."

"Aye, I ken," Declan said, ready to defend his friend. "But Caleb is different. He is like our new laird. He is a good and honorable man. He would have acted in my lady's defense alone."

The priest folded his hands, his face becoming impassive. "I have already sent my servants to gather answers. The man who killed these warriors is, indeed, a bounty hunter, among other things. He comes through the city every so often. On the streets, he's known as the Wolf."

"The Wolf?" Declan said with incredulity. "Forgive me, Father, but truly, ye must be mistaken."

"Wolf? Nay," the wounded MacKintosh warrior said, finding the will to stand. "He's the very devil, himself. He slayed them all, and nearly killed me."

Declan's temper flared. "Ye attacked my lady. Do not feign innocence!"

"No one here is innocent," the priest began, interrupting. He looked Declan hard in the eyes. "Ye gave yer trust too soon. I believe that yer lady is not safe in his care."

Declan tensed. "Why do ye say this, Father?"

"I saw him toss yer lady over his shoulder while she fought for dear life. My men followed them as far as the docks but lost them in the crowd. Sadly, I cannot tell ye where he's taken her."

Declan raked a hand through his hair. "But he is known to me. I have shared meals with him. He must have had a reason for acting so rashly."

The priest's brow furrowed with concern. "I can see the sincerity in yer eyes. Ye have felt a kinship with him, and mayhap he has some redeemable qualities. He is a child of God, after all. Still, I fear he is not a man who can be trusted."

Declan's ears were ringing while he slowly reached into his sporran and withdrew several pieces of silver. His hand shook as he gave them to the priest. "An offering to Saint Columba," he muttered. Then he turned, and on unsteady legs, he made his way back to where his men awaited him.

"What happened? Who did this?" Nachlan asked.

Declan held out his hand, silencing his kinsman's questions. At that moment, he could not speak of what he had learned. His mind raced. Mounting his horse, he took a deep breath, his heart filled with fear as never before. Regret pounded his mind. Lady Tempest was out there in that great city, alone with a man whose character was now in question. The priest was right. Declan had only known Caleb for a brief while, months not years. And what did they truly know of him? Only that he was a bounty hunter, not to mention a nameless man.

Could they have all been led astray by a wolf like a flock of trusting sheep?

But then a memory flashed in his mind of Caleb riding toward the village in the pouring rain with two young children in his arms whom he had rescued from the storm-racked moors.

Declan hesitated. Torn by the conflicting versions of Caleb's character, he had never been so uncertain. He forced himself to set his concern for Caleb aside and turned to his men. "We must find our lady. Her life is in peril!" Urging his horse forward, he took lead. "Move along," he shouted at the people impeding their way.

Declan fought to calm his racing thoughts. He had no choice but to accept the testimony of the priest. Until Caleb could prove otherwise, he was now responsible for the dishonorable death of Laird MacKintosh and for abducting Lady Tempest. Declan only prayed they would find her before Caleb committed another unforgivable misdeed.

Chapter Thirteen

Caleb's brow furrowed with determination as he scanned the streets, searching for Declan. Now that he'd had a chance to cool his ire and reflect on his recent actions, he knew that he had crossed a line.

Hell, he had crossed several lines.

"Damn ye, Nathan," he muttered, once again blaming his friend for his ill fortune. But even as he said the words, he knew he had no one to blame but himself. He had let his self-control slip. Now, it was too late to change all that had occurred. All he could do now was to set his sights on the future.

His future.

Alone.

In his mind's eye, he saw his last glimpse of Tempest before he locked the door, her eyes seething with rage. For a moment, regret stole into his heart, knowing he would never see her again, and her rage would always remain.

But then he squared his shoulders. "'Tis as it should be."

Once he found Declan, he would tell the captain of the Brodie guard where he could find Tempest, and then Caleb would leave Inverness and return to the life he had always known.

He was a bounty hunter after all. Tracking down criminals for a price came naturally to him as did the life that accompanied his occupation. Caleb was accustomed to swordfights, taverns, and crude speech. His bed was warmed by a different woman in whichever town he was in.

He gave his heart to no one—how could he when it didn't come with a name?

From now on, he would ensure his thoughts did not stray from his current mission, which was to find Declan and to get as far from Lady Tempest as he could.

He pushed through the streets with determined purpose, his gaze ever watchful for the Brodie plaid. It was slow going as the road was especially crowded. In the distance, he spied the reason for the delay. Several revelers had dressed as a monstrous snake and were winding through the crowd. They were paying homage to a time centuries before when Saint Columba had miraculously rid the River Ness of an infamous monster that had been terrorizing nearby villagers.

When at last, the procession had moved on to another part of Inverness, Caleb hastened as quickly as he could to Cathedral Square to, once again, check the stables, but when he arrived Declan was still nowhere to be found. Leaving the livery behind, he ducked into an alleyway and circled back around, heading toward the docks. If Declan and the others were in the city, they would have learned soon enough that accommodations were scarce. It was likely that Declan would have done what Caleb had chosen to do upon their arrival in Inverness and find a tavern or brothel, in which to bed down.

Inverness's port was filled with people singing in the streets, their tankards held high. He pushed through the throng, searching the roadsides and businesses for the Brodie plaid.

"Blast," he said as he stepped back outside, having fruitlessly inquired after Declan at another brothel. He looked up at the sky and cursed again, raking his hand through his hair.

Then he cast his gaze to the tavern in which he had locked Tempest away.

He clenched his hands into tight fists. "Damnation!" No doubt, she was beginning to feel the pangs of hunger. If he did not find Declan soon, then he would have no choice but to return to the room, unlock the door, and set eyes on her again.

Was he cursed?

Just when he started to look up to the heavens for an angel to intervene, he glimpsed the blues and greens of the Brodie plaid further up the road.

"Finally," he exclaimed as he hastened forward, but then he hesitated.

How was he going to explain his actions to Declan? He was one of the few men Caleb truly regarded as a friend.

"'Tis of no true consequence," Caleb muttered, shaking his head at his own concern. What Declan thought didn't matter. Just as Tempest was better off without him, so, too, was Declan and the rest of Clan Brodie.

The heaviness of regret settled in his chest as he set out toward the familiar men. How he wished he had never come to Clan Brodie. Then he would never have been bewitched by its reckless lady, nor would he feel the sting of friendships lost.

He drew to a quick halt as a wagon passed in front of him. Craning his neck to see over the merchant and his wares, he kept his gaze trained on his companions.

But suddenly a sharp pain shot through his head.

The blue and green plaids blurred, and the world turned black.

~ * ~

Searing pain blazed like fire behind Caleb's eyes. Groaning, he tried to grip his aching head in his hands. But his arms wouldn't move. Slowly, he lifted his lids only to shut them a moment later as the light blasted his head.

"He's waking up," Caleb heard a man say.

"Leave us," another man replied.

A few moments later, he recognized the sound of a door shutting.

Caleb's nostrils flared as he breathed deeply, then willed his eyes to open. It took a moment for the room to come into focus and longer for Caleb to get his bearings. He was sitting in a simple wooden chair with his hands secured behind his back. The room was clean and sparsely furnished but for the chair he sat in and the one across from him, which was occupied by an older man with a regal bearing who was quietly staring at Caleb. He had silver hair and a beard that was a deeper gray. Both were trimmed short. Caleb's gaze dropped from the man's handsome face, etched with age lines, to the broach on his plaid that had a ruby the size of a plump berry at its center. Caleb's gaze trailed down to the rings lining his long fingers at rest on his knee. Beside him was a simple table, upon which sat two tankards. Caleb's gaze returned to the man's face. His faded blue eyes held curiosity and a quiet confidence.

"My name is Laird Donald Munro," the man said in an unhurried tone. "I would like to offer my apologies for the heavy handed manner of my men."

Caleb was surprised by the man's speech. "Laird?" Caleb grunted, wishing his head would cease pounding. "Ye look like one, but ye sound like an Englishman."

A slight smile curved the older man's lips. "Hardly, but I do sound like a lowlander. I fostered with Clan Maxwell; however, I'm as much a Scotsman and a Highlander as you."

Caleb shrugged. "Ye don't sound like any lowlander I've ever met."

"Let's just say that I've enjoyed a rich education, which has flavored my speech."

Having no wish to continue exchanging pleasantries with the man responsible for attacking and abducting him, Caleb asked the question burning in his aching mind. "What the hell do ye want with me?"

"We'll get to that," Laird Munro said dismissively. "Now then, I've had most of the furnishings removed from the room to minimize the chance of you quickly fashioning a weapon and killing me before my men have time to interfere." He raised a brow at Caleb. "Yer reputation with a sword precedes you."

Caleb shrugged, still wishing he could hold his pounding head in his hands. "I'm better than some."

"So they say," the man said dryly. "I'm not one to typically trust the word of a bounty hunter, but if ye promise not to strike me, then I will release ye. First, however, I must inform ye that my men are just outside the door. I've instructed them to enter and kill you immediately should they fear for a moment that harm could befall me. If you decide to give me your promise, you would do well to honor it and to keep your words and tone respectful."

"Ye seem to have thought of everything," Caleb said absently, as he fought to keep his eyes open against the pain, while he searched his memories for a Laird Munro.

"I usually do," the older man answered.

Caleb grunted again. Normally, he, too, prided himself on his caution and care to detail. But his actions as of late had fallen short of that standard to say the least.

"Well, do I have your promise to behave?"

Caleb nodded, only to wince an instant later. He needed to remember to keep his head still.

"I need your word," Laird Munro insisted.

"Ye have my promise not to hurt ye," Caleb gritted out against the pain.

Keeping his eyes open, despite his throbbing skull, Caleb watched the man stand. He stiffened when the Munro withdrew a slim dirk from his knee-high boot, then walked behind Caleb.

"What are ye about?" Caleb snapped.

Laird Munro gave no reply but seized the bindings securing Caleb's hands together. Then, in a quick move, the ropes fell away.

Without hesitation, Caleb gripped his head in his hands, leaning his elbows on his knees.

"I don't envy the headache ye must have," Laird Munro said. "Here, this will help."

Caleb looked up. The older man offered him one of the tankards. Caleb's mouth was parched, but he did not take the cup.

"You needn't hesitate. It isn't poisoned. If I wanted you dead, you would be so already."

Caleb couldn't argue with his logic, nor could he deny his thirst any longer or the relief his head might feel from the drink. Accepting the cup, he brought it to his lips. Smelling naught but ale, he drank it down in one long draught.

"Have another," the man said, taking the empty tankard from Caleb's hand and replacing it with a full one. This time Caleb took a long sip and then sat back for a moment, letting his eyes close. After several more sips, the pain began to lessen enough that he no longer wished to carve the eyes from his head.

Meeting Laird Munro's gaze, Caleb repeated his question. "What do ye want with me?"

Laird Munro eased back in his chair and gave Caleb a scrutinizing look before he said, "Recently, you have been seen with a lady, on several occasions in fact."

Caleb stiffened at the mention of Tempest. He sat straight and gave the man a hard look. "What concern is my lady to ye?"

Laird Munro canted his head, giving Caleb a curious look. "She didn't tell you about me?"

Caleb did not reply at first. Who was this man? At length, he simply said, "Nay."

A glint shone in his eyes. "I'm not surprised. She's a reckless lass and given to whimsy."

Caleb did not like hearing this man speak so familiarly of Tempest. He fought to keep his tone level. The last thing he wanted was to be charged by this man's loyal guards intent on killing first and asking questions after. "Ye still have not told me who ye are."

Laird Munro smiled. "As a matter of fact, I'm the lady's betrothed."

It was all Caleb could do to hide his surprise. What was this man playing at? Tempest was no more betrothed than Caleb was the son of a laird. He gave the older man a pointed look. "Her family has never spoken of ye."

Laird Munro cast his gaze heavenward for a moment. "I should have guessed as much." He shifted his gaze back to Caleb's. "I was chosen by her father, but after his death, her family has sought not to honor the match because of our age difference."

Doubt suddenly crept into Caleb's thoughts. Certainly, Caleb knew that Tempest's older sister, Elora, would have done everything to fight the match had it been made by their father.

"Still," the older man continued. "She has wished to honor our contract, or at least she told me as much."

Caleb did not know what to say. Was it possible that Tempest and this man were, indeed, betrothed?

Laird Munro sat back in his seat with a look of resignation on his face. "None of this matters now, not if she has given her heart to you." The older man gave Caleb an expectant look. "Well, has she?"

Caleb stiffened, sitting alert, more confused than ever. "Has she what?"

Laird Munro raised his brow at Caleb. "I thought I spoke plainly enough but allow me to get right to the point. Is she in love with you?"

Caleb could not guess at the man's game. Keeping his face impassive, he lifted his shoulders, and said casually, "She is young."

To Caleb's surprise, Laird Munro's countenance softened. "She is that," he said, smiling gently. An absent look came into his eyes. "So, too, was my wife when we first wed. But she loved me with all her heart, and I loved her from the very first moment I saw her. She was a spitfire, my wife, like our lady. Strong. Opinionated. And I loved nothing more than to listen to every word she ever spoke."

Caleb did not doubt the man's sincerity. "What happened to her?"

Laird Munro paused for a moment. It was clear that it still pained him to speak of her. "She was taken from me not five years after we wed." His voice dropped as he continued. "Her carriage was attacked by thieves. The driver tried to outrun the bandits, but the carriage overturned...breaking her neck. My children were also lost."

Silence hung in the air.

"May God rest their souls," Caleb said quietly.

Slowly, light returned to the man's gaze. "'Twas long ago. I never remarried, but in recent years I thought to remedy this. I know our lady does not love me, but I hoped her affection would grow in time." A sad smile curved Laird Munro's lips. "'Tis the wish of every old man, I suppose." He cleared his throat and looked hard at Caleb. "But I will see that she is happy, even if it's not with me. Now then, I know she has given her heart to you. Do you deny this?"

Caleb suddenly felt like an animal backed in a corner. "I...er..."

Laird Munro did not wait for Caleb to answer. "And you love her, do you not?"

Caleb raked a hand through his hair. "'Tis not as easy as that."

Laird Munro nodded. "It never is with her. She's given to mischief and is, at times, selfish—"

"She is not!" Caleb snapped, straightening in his chair, but remembering the men waiting outside to kill him, he dropped his voice. "She is kind and loyal and passionate!"

Laird Munro gave him a knowing look. "So you do love her."

At that moment, Caleb realized that he had walked right into Laird Munro's trap. He shrugged and sat back. "Like I said, 'tis not as easy as that. I have no title, no land."

Laird Munro waved his hand in a careless gesture. "Your protest is easily remedied. I will give you land and a title; that is, if she chooses you."

Caleb raised a brow at him. "Forgive me if I doubt yer sincerity."

Laird Munro leaned forward, his gaze suddenly intense. "Listen to me and listen well, lad. When my beloved died, my heart did not just break, my very soul died. I wouldn't wish such pain on anyone. But I had the solace of knowing she was among the angels and that I would see her again when I ventured into the hereafter." His brows drew together, his expression pained. He placed a hand over his heart. "Even having experienced such loss, I cannot imagine a greater hell than one where she yet walked this earth but without me by her side." His hands shifted, gripping the arms of his chair. "Do you understand that if you were to deny your hearts, you would be condemning each other to hell, each new day worse than the last. You will both go to bed at night and stare up at the ceiling, longing for the other. But she will have another man lying in your place. She will give birth to children not born of love but of duty."

"I...I only want what's best for her. She deserves a laird."

"You speak words of honor," The older man scoffed. "But 'tis a cruel, bleak future you've planned for her." Laird Munro moved to sit on the edge of his seat, his gaze boring into Caleb's. "How quickly will that fire we both admire be snuffed out by a loveless union?"

Caleb closed his eyes against the vision that came to his mind of a tired, lackluster Tempest, living in a cold and barren castle. "Nay," he snapped, shaking away his imaginings. "Ye know not of what ye speak! She cannot marry me!"

"And why not?" Laird Munro demanded.

"I've already said why. She is a lady. I am a commoner." Caleb could feel his control unraveling.

"That is your fear talking!"

"That is the truth!"

"I have already offered you land and title. Still, you would deny her."

Caleb stood, his fists clenched. "I don't deserve her!"

An instant later, the door flung wide and men with swords brandished high rushed at Caleb, but Laird Munro lunged in front of him, shielding Caleb with his body.

"Stand down," the older man bellowed.

The guards skidded to a stop, the ones in the rear colliding with the leaders. Without comment or complaint, they bowed their heads to their laird, then turned and left the room.

Caleb released the tension from his stance. Breathless, Laird Munro turned to face Caleb. "Whether or not you deserve her is not for you to decide. That decision is hers, alone."

"Nay," Caleb protested, but Laird Munro seized his tunic in his fists and pulled him close and looked him hard in the eye.

"If you are lucky enough to find love—you seize it! You guard it close, and you fight to the death to keep it!"

Something Caleb could not identify bloomed in his heart. Mayhap, it was hope, but he knew better than to allow its seed to take root. He released the breath he'd been holding. "Ye're mad," Caleb said dismissively.

Laird Munro's hands dropped to his sides. In an instant, he regained his composure and stood before Caleb with all the grace and dignity of his station. "I assure you that my mind is quite sound. I told you—I only want her to be happy. If that means marrying you, then I will not rest until I see that done." Laird Munro cleared his throat. "Come. We will go and speak with her now."

Caleb shook his head, his heart pounding. "I...I have to think about all this."

Laird Munro smiled. "Forgive me, I have not made myself clear. You have no choice. Her happiness is my priority. If she wants you, you will marry her."

The last time Caleb had seen Tempest her eyes blazed with anger. Caleb rubbed the back of his neck. "Before today, she might have chosen me, but I do not think I still have her favor."

"There is only one way to find out." Laird Munro gestured for Caleb to follow as he opened the door. Stepping into the hallway, Caleb was not surprised to see six warriors with their swords unsheathed.

Laird Munro held out his hands. "Put away your weapons. He is not a threat."

The men immediately acquiesced and stepped back to give Laird Munro and Caleb space to pass. Caleb followed him down the hallway. They passed several doors but stopped in front of a door guarded by two Munro warriors.

Laird Munro locked eyes with Caleb. "Are you ready to speak from the heart?"

Caleb glanced at the warriors before shifting his gaze back the way they'd come. Then he leaned past the Munro and looked further down the hallway. He saw a landing, and a young maid carrying a tray down the hall toward the opposite wing. Nothing looked familiar.

Confused, Caleb once again met Laird Munro's gaze. "But she isn't here," he said in a low voice, not wishing to embarrass the laird in front of his men.

Mayhap Laird Munro was, indeed, mad.

The older man's composure never wavered. "I assure you that she is."

Caleb raised a brow at him. "But I'm quite certain she is not."

Laird Munro smiled. "Trust me. I heard her yelling to be released a short while before you arrived. She's quite angry. But as you've come to learn as well, the only way to ensure her safety is to keep her under lock and key."

Caleb's brow drew together. "But...I locked her in a room in another tavern. There's no way she could have gotten out."

Laird Munro chuckled. "Do ye think it wise to underestimate her? As you can see, I have two guards stationed here. I also have two more outside her window, and I still wouldn't be surprised were she to escape."

Caleb nodded begrudgingly. "I see yer point." He took a deep breath and looked at the door, behind which Tempest no doubt paced the room, fuming with anger.

But then a new thought occurred to Caleb. Did he not have cause for anger? These months have passed, and all the while she has been betrothed to another man and never told him.

He swallowed a growl of frustration. Ever since he'd met Tempest, life had become complicated and unpredictable. This only proved that his instincts had been right. He needed to get as far away from her as he could.

But then his mind was bombarded by Laird Munro's words...*If you are lucky enough to find love—you seize it!*

But how could he seize love, when he'd just found out that she was betrothed to another man, a laird no less? And Laird Munro did say that she had sought to honor their contract.

But then why had she never mentioned this fact to him?

Or had her intentions changed when she met Caleb?

But how could that be possible? Surely, she would want to marry a powerful laird over a lowly born nothing like him.

Still, Laird Munro had just promised him land and a title.

He clenched his jaw. His mind was spinning out of control.

"Enough," Laird Munro snapped, drawing Caleb's gaze. "I see you weighing matters still in your mind." The older man clamped his hand on Caleb's shoulder. "You're afraid. I can see that. But your fear is trying to protect your heart. Don't listen. Fear is a liar. Fear cannot be your guide through this life. If you listen to it, you will never truly know what it means to love and be loved in return." Laird Munro pointed to the door. "Choose courage. Choose love. Before it's too late!"

Caleb's heart pounded. He closed his eyes and felt Tempest's gentle kiss on his back and heard her whisper..."*When will ye learn that I do what I want. And what I want is ye.*"

He stood straighter. Tempest wanted *him*!

How could anything else matter more?

His eyes flew open. "Ye're right!" He turned and pounded his fist on the door. "Tempest! Tempest, 'tis I!" He faltered for a moment, then pushed through his fear. "The world be damned! I love ye, Tempest! I have loved ye from the very start." He pressed his forehead to the door. "Well, I wanted ye from the start, but when ye tripped on the bucket in the stables...that was the moment. And damn yer spirit and yer recklessness—Despite how I've scolded ye, they made me love ye all the more. I...I see the woman ye are destined to be. A great woman—that is what ye are!" He shifted his gaze and looked Laird Munro hard in the eye. "Open the damn door!"

The laird chuckled. "Tempest...'tis an apt pet name to be sure." He drew a key from his sporran and unlocked the door.

A woman with ropes of flaxen hair, wide green eyes, and delicate features stood with her arms open. "I love ye," she vowed to Caleb, her voice trembling with emotion.

Stunned, Caleb slammed the door. He whirled around and locked eyes with the laird. "I've never seen that woman before in my life! Where's Tempest?"

The warm smile disappeared from Laird Munro's face. "What are you playing at?"

"Me!" Caleb growled. "Ye've deceived me!"

The laird's guards withdrew their swords, but Caleb's anger overcame his caution. "Tell yer men to step down. Ye've toyed with my heart enough."

Laird Munro shook his head with contempt. "You choose the cowards way then. You would deny her your heart?"

Caleb narrowed his eyes. "I choose my way, and my lady—which that woman is not! Ye told me to fight to the death for the woman I love, and so I shall! Ye now stand between me and that lady. What is yer choice, Laird Munro? Will ye stand down, or will *ye* stand in love's way?"

Laird Munro's eyes were cold, but he shrugged as if to show how little Caleb now meant. "If 'tis another you love, then you do not deserve my lady's heart." He pursed his lips and shook his head slightly at his men who dropped their swords and stepped to one side, giving Caleb room to pass.

He didn't hesitate.

He hastened from the inn and stepped outside. Caleb took a deep breath, hoping the fresh air would help clear his senses. His head pounded. He had no idea what Laird Munro had truly wanted from him, but one thing was certain—the old man had succeeded in planting more than just a seed in Caleb's mind. He had revealed to Caleb his own folly.

Tempest loved him.

He loved her.

He would not waste another moment upholding conventions or laws. Such rules were for other men. Men with something to lose.

Caleb had nothing to lose, except for the love of his life. And he'd be damned before he'd let that happen.

With an intensity of purpose he had never known, he barreled down the road. Nothing was going to stop him now.

"Ye bastard!"

Except for the three MacKintosh warriors who now blocked his path, their faces twisted with rage.

"Damnation!" Caleb growled, fighting the urge to plow through the men with swinging fists. "Give up already!" Caleb snapped. "Clan MacKintosh cannot win against Clan Brodie!"

The man in the middle stepped forward. His eyes filled with loathing. "Ye saw to that, didn't ye," he sneered before he dropped a gauntlet at Caleb's feet. "The glade in the woods beyond the city walls. Be there anon. 'Tis a fight to the death."

Before Caleb could reply to say that he had no wish to fight, the men turned on their heels and marched away.

"'Tis not my concern," he said aloud and continued forward.

Clan MacKintosh did not matter.

Nor did Laird Munro and his betrothed.

The only thing that mattered was releasing Tempest, apologizing from the very depths of his heart, and pledging his undying love for her.

He only prayed that her love for him ran deep enough to forgive him.

Chapter Fourteen

Tempest lay on the bed, staring up at the high ceiling. Her gaze absently traced the crossbeams while her thoughts darted from one image of Caleb to another.

From the kind moments to the cruel ones.

She thought of his quiet confidence and steady ways. Her heart lingered when a breathless memory came to her. The moment when she had stood close to him in the stables, so close that she could smell his skin and feel the heat flow off his body. Moments such as that had been few but were so powerful that they filled her soul and planted an ache in her heart, which the passing of time had not been able to soothe. She longed to touch that Caleb, to run her fingers down his scarred back and heal the wounds the eye could not see.

But how could she reconcile that Caleb with the one she now knew? The one with a blood thirsty temper who had made love to another woman and locked her away, not once but twice.

With a screech, she stood and began pacing the room.

Who was this man?

How could he be so controlled one moment and so ruthless the next? What did he have to gain by his actions?

She crossed the room and stared down at the cold hearth. In that moment, she wished she could take back her heart, or better yet that she had never set eyes on Caleb in the first place.

But anger gave her no comfort.

She felt hollow inside. Hollow and alone.

She slumped on the bed and covered her face with her hands, fighting the urge to scream her fury and confusion to the ceiling. Tears stung her eyes.

"Nay!" she snapped, scolding herself.

She would not cry, not for him, not after he had betrayed her. How could she? Still, despite her protests, tears ran down her cheeks.

Then she heard a key being inserted in the lock. Her breath caught. She jerked her hands away from her eyes and whirled to face the door.

Click.

"Oh God," she breathed, her heart pounding.

The door opened. Caleb stood in the doorway. Their eyes locked, and the emotion poured out of her before she could check herself.

Her face crumpled. "I loved ye," she cried.

In an instant, he was there, pulling her into his arms, soothing her tears.

"Nay," she screeched, pushing him away.

"Please," he said softly, holding her close despite her struggles.

"I despise ye," she blurted.

"I'm sorry," he crooned. His soft lips brushed her ear.

"Nay," she railed. "I need to hate ye." She pounded her fist on his chest.

Taking her blows without flinching, he whispered. "Ye don't hate me."

She pushed against his chest. "Damn it! Let me go!"

His blue eyes searched hers. "Tell me ye don't love me, and I will let ye go," he said, his voice husky.

She couldn't.

A slow, sensual smiled curved his mouth to one side. He crushed her against him. His lips descended, claiming hers. She moaned, desperate and hurting. Her heart thundered in her chest. She tried to resist, but then as if of their own accord, her arms encircled his neck. She clung to him. He raked his hands possessively down her back, coursing over her hips. His tongue plunged into her mouth, hungry, searching. He held nothing back. He was wild and raw, igniting her own desire. Instinct took over. The ache consumed her. She lost herself to the power of his unrestrained touch. With a growl that set her aching body on fire, he jerked his shirt over his head, swept her off her feet, and laid her down on the bed. An instant later, he covered her. Her hands gripped his back, then caressed his smooth skin—

She froze.

Her eyes flew open. Fear cut straight to her pounding heart.

"What is it, my love?" the man on top of her said as he trailed kisses across her cheek. "Ye've gone stiff as a board. Where's my wildcat?"

She swallowed hard, unable to speak. All she could hear was her heart pounding in ears. Finally, she blurted. "Ye're not Caleb!"

Caleb's face hovered above her, but the arrogant smile that curved his lips would never belong to her love. "I'm whoever ye want me to be for the next hour," the man drawled.

"Get off me," she screamed, thrashing her legs and pushing against his chest with all her might.

A cold laugh met her ears. "Now, this is more like it. I much prefer rough play over tender love." The man pinned her hands down on the bed. "Don't play the virgin with me. No innocent has ever kissed the way ye do. I may not be this Caleb ye fancy, but my body is hard, yers is ripe, and the evening is long."

"Nay," she cried. "Get off me! Caleb," she screamed. "Caleb!"

Just then a loud banging shook the door. "Wolf," a man shouted.

Tempest ceased her struggles. A hardness settled in the familiar features above her, making him almost unrecognizable.

Surely, Caleb's eyes had never been so cold.

"Damn it," the man growled and rolled off her. Then he stood and crossed to the door, giving Tempest a clear view of his unblemished, muscular back. She stared in horror at his perfect skin.

The man threw open the door. "This had better be important."

A giant of a man with a scraggly beard and greasy hair stepped into the room. His lustful gaze raked over her, making her stomach sick. She sat up and hugged her knees to her chest.

"What?" the Caleb imitator snapped, drawing the ugly man's gaze.

In his beefy hand, he held up a gauntlet. "Ye've been called out to a duel."

"What fool is this?" her abductor asked, his tone cold and impassive.

"Ye killed a laird today. His men aren't happy about it."

His smooth, sinewy shoulders shrugged. "What are the terms?"

"Ye're to meet them outside the city limits. 'Tis a fight to the death."

"What are the spoils if I win?" His voice was cold and calculating and sent a shiver up her spine.

The big man laughed. "If ye win? Don't ye mean when?"

Her captor did not laugh in return. Instead, he looked at her, his expression hard and unreadable.

What was happening?

Was she dreaming?

Please God, let this be a nightmare from which she would wake.

When she thought she could bear his emotionless appraisal no longer, he said, "I think I will take it all if I win. The chiefdom, the clan's coffers, and ye my lady."

Her nostrils flared as she swallowed the defiant urge to inform him that she was not of Clan MacKintosh, and that he could best every one of Egan's warriors in battle and still would have no claim over her; however, she somehow managed to hold her tongue. Afterall, the less he knew of her true identity, the better.

She held back the smirk that tugged at her lips. In his arrogance, he had not even asked her name.

He bent to the floor and seized his tunic. Then he crossed to the bedside. "This is far from over," he said, his voice low. Her breath stuck in her chest. He looked so much like Caleb as he hovered above her. His hair was slightly longer, but otherwise, there was no perceptible difference between the two men...other than their characters and their backs.

He leaned over and planted a kiss on her lips. It was all she could do to silence her fighting spirit, but she held her tongue and kept her body still.

"I won't be gone long, my lady. I'm just going to kill some men. When I return, we can resume where we left off." Then he straightened, his tunic still clenched in his hand.

She swallowed the string of fiery insults.

Just go, her mind screamed.

Her gaze followed his flawless back out the door. When, at last, she was alone, she scurried off the bed and stood there for a moment, her body frozen, her mind racing, her heart pounding.

How was it possible?

Caleb had never mentioned having a brother.

And then a smile broke across her face and her heart soared.

The imposter had done all those things.

Caleb had never dallied in the stables with some unknown strumpet. He never stabbed Egan in the back. He was not even the one who had locked her away—at least the second time.

But just as quickly as her smile had appeared, it vanished.

Someone who looked like Caleb was responsible.

What if others assumed what she had? Worse yet, what if Caleb did not know he had a twin brother? What if the ruthless Caleb, who was lethal with a sword, found out about the real Caleb?

With a screech, she raced to the door and began pounding the slatted wood with her fists, demanding her freedom.

"Please let me out," she begged.

Then, wincing as pain shot up her arms, she turned and slid to the ground. Hugging her aching hands to her chest, she scanned the room with determination.

Somehow, someway, she needed to escape and find the real Caleb before it was too late.

Chapter Fifteen

Caleb's sharp gaze scanned the passersby as he hastened down the road, which was lined with taverns and brothels on both sides. The pungent scent of low tide filled the air, while the sound of merriment and the din of sailors unloading their cargo blasted his ears. Despite the surrounding chaos his thoughts wove like ribbons around images that flashed in his mind's eye—Tempest's penetrating blue gaze, the feel of her waist as he held her close, his heart wanting, needing yet always resisting.

He straightened his shoulders. Now, he was done resisting.

But then he faltered. His pace slowed. Like a knife that cut through his heart to his very soul, another image came to the fore of his thoughts.

Cold eyes, hard and narrow. Calloused hands gripping a whip. A look of disgust on his father's face.

Ye're nothin', lad. Good for nothin'!

The words tore through Caleb's mind again and again as phantom pain shot through his body, radiating out from his back to the very tips of his fingers, stealing his breath.

He stopped in his tracks. His mind racing. What was he doing? He had no right to claim Tempest as his own.

He didn't deserve her.

"Nay," Caleb growled aloud, fighting the devil talking in his mind.

He would listen to demons no longer!

He broke into a sprint, weaving and dodging through the crowded street. His arms pumped as he raced to outrun the pain and doubt.

When he saw The Crescent Moon, he drew to a stop.

Breathless, he bent over, his hands on his knees. Images of blue eyes and declarations of love fought for dominance over bashing fists and stinging words.

This was the moment—the test of his lifetime.

For so many years, he had held tight to his control, seldom surrendering to anger or impulse and never giving himself to love. Solitude had always been his destiny, never dreaming that he could find fulfillment or joy.

He stood straight. "Not anymore," he pledged and threw open the door to The Crescent Moon. With courage and love filling his heart, he marched across the common room floor.

"Nachlan, now!" a familiar voice snapped, drawing Caleb's gaze. He locked eyes with Declan an instant before a sword was pointed at his heart.

Caleb glanced at the man who threatened his life. "Hello, Nachlan." Then he shifted his gaze back to the captain of the Brodie guard. There was a hard set to Declan's jaw and no warmth in his eyes.

"Explain yerself?" Declan demanded.

Caleb pressed his lips together in a grim line. Judging by the fact that Declan was looking at him as if he were the son of the Devil, Caleb was left to assume that he must have already heard Tempest's account of the last two days.

Declan stepped closer, his eyes menacing. "I will ask ye only one time more. Explain yerself."

Caleb knew he needed Tempest's forgiveness, but he hadn't counted on having to repent to her clan, too. With his arms at his sides, he took a deep breath. He would do whatever it took to regain her trust. "I ken that I've acted without honor," Caleb said for all to hear.

"Then ye admit it," Nachlan growled, pressing his sword into Caleb's flesh.

"Aye," Caleb said simply without wincing, despite the pricking pain. "I will accept the consequences of my actions."

"The consequences of yer actions," Declan repeated, his voice bewildered. "We cannot begin to know what the ramifications will be. Ye've very well started a war!"

"Pardon?" Caleb asked surprised.

"Ye heard me," Declan snapped.

Caleb scanned the Brodie warrior's furious faces, looking for a single ally. "I'm certainly not dismissing what I've done. Still, starting a war seems rather farfetched."

"Och, do ye believe this one?" a woman said, her voice dripping with disdain.

Caleb's heart lifted when he saw Mary step out from behind Declan, despite the anger etched on her face. He searched the common room for Tempest but did not see her. "Mary," he said in a rush. "Go get Lady Tempest."

Mary's eyes shot daggers of hatred at him as she crossed her arms over her chest. "The last time *I* saw Lady Tempest, she was slung over yer shoulder after we caught ye dallying with that blonde floozy in the stables and ye shoved poor Henry to the ground!"

Alarms went off in Caleb's head. "What?" He started to walk toward her, but Nachlan warned him not to move by pressing the blade into his skin.

He met Nachlan's gaze and held his hands up as if in surrender. "I don't know what she's talking about."

Mary gasped. "Liar!"

"Ye're not in yer right mind," Caleb said quickly. "Mayhap ye need to lie down."

Mary's eyes flashed with anger. "Do not speak to me as if I'm some kind of adle-minded simpleton. I ken what I saw. Ye killed all those men, not that I'm going to grieve for a single one. And when Henry and I tried to save Tempest from yer fury, ye pushed the lad—barely more than a child—to the ground."

"What?" Caleb could not believe what he was hearing. "I...I—"

"She's not the only one who saw ye," Declan added grimly.

Dumbstruck, Caleb met his friend's gaze. "Ye think I did those things, that I killed people. Who? Who did I kill?"

"Ye stabbed Egan in the back," Declan replied.

Caleb shook his head in disbelief. "Egan MacKintosh?"

"He was a blackguard," Nachlan hissed, drawing Caleb's gaze. "And a thorn in Clan Brodie's side—"

"Nachlan, do not speak ill of the dead," Declan admonished. "We've had enough misfortune as it is."

"Ye're right," Nachlan conceded. "But despite how he was in life, still, 'tis no way for any man to die."

"I didn't kill anyone," Caleb protested.

"Enough," Declan snapped. "Ye've already confessed to acting without honor."

"Aye, I did confess but not to killing anyone or shoving a child or—" He looked at Mary forgetting her other accusation.

"We caught ye knee deep in some lady's skirts!"

"Nor did I do that," he said adamantly. He could feel his own eyes bulging from their sockets. "What I did do was lose all control, and I told Tempest that I love her, ardently. And I kissed her, not for the first time, even though I swore to myself that I would never do it again. But I did, and then I locked her in a room upstairs, despite her protests, only to anger her. Albeit at the time, I felt as though I was doing the right thing. But I have since understood the folly of my actions." He looked beseechingly at Declan. "These are my crimes and only these."

"Bind his hands," Declan snapped.

Caleb's heart raced as he searched for his escape while three Brodie warriors closed in on him.

"Wait," Mary shouted.

Everyone froze. She was a woman who was clearly accustomed to handling unruly men.

"Out of my way," she said gruffly to the Brodie warriors blocking her path.

Even Nachlan stepped aside, allowing Mary to stand in front of Caleb. Slowly, she reached out her hand and cupped Caleb's cheek. Her scrutinizing gaze bore into his. He resisted the urge to push her hand away. Instead, he held her gaze without flinching.

After several tense moments, her face softened. "Ye don't lie beneath as many men as I have and not be able to tell when one is lying." She looked back at Declan and lifted her shoulders. "Mayhap the man I saw only bore a strong resemblance to him." Her gaze trailed down Caleb's person. "The man I saw wasn't wearing a plaid."

Caleb held up his hands. "I've no other clothes. Ye saw for yerself when I came here."

Declan drew closer, giving Mary a hard look. "Are ye doubting what ye saw?"

Mary paused. Then, at length, she nodded.

Declan's brow furrowed. "Then ye're no longer certain?"

Mary's nostrils flared as she considered Caleb. "I know what I saw, but...mayhap..." She blew out a long breath. "Aye, I'm no longer certain." But then her gaze narrowed on Caleb. She thrust a finger in his face. "None of this proves yer innocence."

"Tempest can prove my innocence. Go get her from yer room," Caleb demanded.

"She's not there," Mary replied.

"What do ye mean she's not there?" A dark feeling of foreboding crept around Caleb's heart.

Declan stepped forward. "Ye don't know where she is?" he said to Caleb, his eyes wide with fear.

"Of course I do," Caleb snapped. "I already told ye that I locked her in Mary's room." He pushed past Nachlan, bounding up the stairs.

"I helped her escape," Mary called after him. "She's not there."

Caleb froze. His heart renewed its pounding. He turned back around, taking in the ashen look on his companion's faces. "Then none of us knows where Tempest is?"

"Mother of God help us," Declan prayed.

Caleb's nostrils flared. "The MacKintosh!"

"I told ye," Declan began. "Egan is dead, and more witnesses than Mary claim the deed was done by yer hand."

"'Tis a lie," Caleb said with a snarl of frustration. "We're wasting time!"

"I am willing to allow ye to prove yer innocence," Declan said stepping forward. "Only Tempest can clear yer name now."

Anger tore through Caleb. "My name means nothing," he growled. "The only thing that matters is finding her." He looked Declan hard in the eye. "We must find her!"

Declan held out a calming hand. "Aye, but she could be anywhere. Where do we start looking?"

"We can go from tavern to tavern and gather information," Mary said, chiming in. "Someone is bound to know where she's being held."

Caleb shook his head. "That will take too long." His thoughts went directly to the gauntlet dropped at his feet earlier. Clearly, the MacKintosh warrior who challenged him to a duel believed that Caleb had killed his laird. Mayhap he knew where to find Tempest.

He turned to Declan. "A fight to the death—that is where we begin our search."

~ * ~

Caleb rode behind Declan as they passed through the gate, leaving Inverness behind. Nachlan flanked him on one side, and Hamish, a tall warrior with thick, wavy brown hair, broad shoulders, and a reserved countenance, rode on Caleb's other side. Both men's jaws were set with grim determination. It did not escape Caleb's notice that he was being guarded, but he didn't care.

He was not concerned over Nachlan's cool manner, nor was he bothered by the suspicious glances Declan kept throwing over his shoulder at him—how could he be when, by all accounts a brutal swordsman, who strongly resembled Caleb in appearance had single-handedly slaughtered several MacKintosh warriors, including their laird, and abducted the woman he loved?

"Blast!" he cursed under his breath. If only he had allowed his heart to be his guide the night before. He closed his eyes for a moment and remembered Tempest declaring her ardent regard for him. Regret ate at his soul. At the time, he had believed that by ensuring she married a nobleman he was doing the honorable thing—putting her wellbeing above his own heart. How wrong he had been. What he should have done was sweep her into his arms and bang on the door of every kirk and chapel in the city until one of the priests could be persuaded to marry them on the spot.

Then, he would know exactly where Tempest was at that moment.

As his wife, she would have been safe and warm in his arms.

They reached a thick wood, forcing their party to shift into a single line with Declan still leading and Hamish directly behind Caleb. The forest was cooler and filled with an earthy scent made of decaying logs and moss, combined with fresh tones like green leaves and ferns splayed wide to catch the slivers of sunlight through the trees. But Caleb could not breathe in the perfumed air or see the dancing lights. His surroundings felt as heavy and hazy as his mind.

Declan drew his horse to a halt and turned back to face Caleb, forcing his thoughts out of the fog of regret and into the present.

"The clearing is up ahead." Declan said to Caleb. For a moment the older man looked him hard in the eye. Caleb did not flinch under his scrutiny. He knew he had nothing to hide.

At length, Declan asked. "Did ye kill Egan?"

"Ye already know my answer," Caleb replied simply.

Hamish cleared his throat, drawing their gazes. His face had softened slightly as he said to Declan, "We've been training with Caleb for some time now. He's a skilled swordsman to be sure but no prize fighter. He could never defeat so many warriors at once."

Declan blew out a long breath. "Unless that's what he wanted us to believe all along."

Doubt once more shadowed Hamish's face.

Declan shook his head. "We've still proven nothing." Declan looked off into the distance for a moment, then turned and once more met Caleb's gaze. "Ye can't go into that glade unarmed, but remember, we're watching ye." Declan called back to one of the warriors who had several swords wrapped in a plaid that was strapped to the back of his horse. "Give him a blade."

Nachlan, who was in line behind Hamish, spoke up. "Are ye certain that is wise?"

Declan shook his head. "There is little of which I am certain, but none of us knows what awaits us in that clearing. I will not lead an unarmed man to his death."

The sword was passed from one warrior to the next; until Hamish took it. He paused for a moment. It was clear the warrior was still considering whether Caleb should be trusted with the blade. By all accounts whomever killed Egan had single-handedly bested several MacKintosh warriors himself. Caleb knew Hamish was worried that with a sword in hand, he would somehow best them, too. Despite wanting to reassure Hamish and defend his own character, Caleb kept his silence. Until they found Tempest, who could attest to his innocence, he would have to tolerate everyone's suspicions.

"Hamish, I gave ye an order," Declan said, his voice firm.

Hamish nodded and offered Caleb the weapon.

"Thank you," Caleb said simply.

"Before we go any further," Declan began, "I want to make sure ye're ready."

Gripping the sword, Caleb took a deep breath. His thoughts had been so focused on finding Tempest that he hadn't truly reflected on the imminent encounter with Clan MacKintosh. Caleb had never been called out to a duel. He certainly would prefer not to fight and had no wish to take anyone's life. Still, he would do whatever it took to save Tempest. If he had to kill his challenger to do so, then so be it.

He stretched his neck from side to side, then gave a nod to Declan to show that he was ready. With a grim nod in return, Declan urged his horse forward. Caleb followed right behind, and soon, the dense oak and pines gave way to slender birch trees and low bushes. And then they rode into a vast clearing. On the far side, a dozen MacKintosh warriors on horseback were assembled, forming a half moon shape.

Caleb's first thought was that Clan Brodie was outnumbered. His second thought was that Clan MacKintosh had come for vengeance. Hatred poured from their menacing gazes as they all gripped weapons at the ready.

Caleb's gaze settled on the rider in the middle, recognizing him as the one who had dropped the gauntlet. A blood thirsty grin curved the man's lips. He showed no signs of fear but seemed to relish the idea of dueling with Caleb. The warrior dismounted and moved to stand in the center of the glade.

Caleb looked at Declan.

The older man's blue eyes filled with concern. "Should ye choose to fight him, we cannot interfere. Do ye ken?"

Caleb nodded. "I'm hoping it does not come down to a fight. I only wish to glean what he knows about Tempest."

"Go with God," Declan said quietly.

Caleb nodded. Dismounting, he stepped toward the fierce warrior. All the while, he racked his brain for a way to prove his innocence or at least dispel some of the man's anger.

"Hold," someone called out through the trees.

Caleb froze and scanned the edge of the glade, straining to see who had spoken. Suddenly, the clomping of horses' hooves erupted from every direction in the woods beyond the glade. A choir of tree branches and rustling leaves filled the air. A moment later, another band of warriors flooded the clearing, surrounding them all.

Now both Clan Brodie and Clan MacKintosh were outnumbered.

"Caleb, who are these men?" Declan hissed, his weapon held at the ready.

Caleb scanned their number for their leader. His eyes flashed wide when his gaze settled on Laird Munro. "What are ye doing here?"

"Caleb, are ye in league with these men?" Declan said, his voice raising. "Answer me!"

Caleb turned to the captain of the Brodie guard. "Nay, I swear. He abducted me earlier. 'Tis a long story," he said in a rush before shifting his attention back to the Munro.

"Good eventide," Laird Munro said hospitably as he dismounted, joining Caleb and the MacKintosh warrior in the center of the glade.

Caleb's challenger gave the Munro a fierce scowl. "My name is Alan MacKintosh. I came here to avenge my laird. Whoever ye are, ye've no business here."

"On the contrary, I need to speak with this man," the Munro said politely, gesturing to Caleb.

"I will not—" The MacKintosh started to say, but Laird Munro raised a hand. An instant later, the Munro warriors drew their blades. Alan's nostrils flared, and his scowl deepened. Still, he held his tongue.

No one could argue that Laird Munro now had the upper hand.

"How did ye know where to find me?" Caleb asked.

"Naturally, my men followed you," Laird Munro said. "You see, after I spoke with my betrothed, it occurred to me that I had abducted the wrong man—"

"I believe we've already established that," he said interrupting.

"But also, the right man."

Caleb shook his head impatiently. "Ye're confused, old man."

Laird Munro's gaze narrowed with intensity. "I need to know who you are?"

"He's the Wolf," Alan growled. "He killed my laird!"

Caleb shot the MacKintosh an incredulous look. "The Wolf?"

"Then...then you are the Wolf?" Laird Munro stammered.

"What are ye talking about?" Caleb said, his frustration mounting.

"Is this true?" Declan asked, urging his horse into the center, drawing Caleb's gaze. "Are ye the Wolf?"

Caleb shook his head at them all. "What the bloody hell is everyone talking about?"

"Ye're the Wolf!" Alan shouted. "Admit it!"

"I'm not the Wolf," Caleb snapped.

"Damn right he's not." A deep voice said. "I'm the Wolf."

Caleb turned and peered between the Munro warriors on horseback and glimpsed a man, whose features were identical to his own, step into the glade. Behind him followed a band of rough-looking men.

Caleb froze. He could not speak or breathe.

For a moment, everyone was silent.

Then Declan blew out a long breath. "This certainly explains a great deal."

Meanwhile, Caleb's confusion had reached new heights. He and this man were alike in every way, except for the clothing they wore, Caleb in his Brodie plaid and the Wolf in a pair of fitted black hose and black tunic.

"He's stolen yer face," one of the Wolf's men snarled.

The Wolf's gaze narrowed menacingly on Caleb whose limbs felt heavy as if he was fashioned of stone, frozen like a statue in a courtyard—only unbeknownst to everyone, including himself, the artist had carved a replica.

But this copy mirrored Caleb only in appearance, for he could tell by the malice in the Wolf's eyes that he was a hard and dangerous man.

Chapter Sixteen

Tempest stared down from her casement at the tops of the heads of two men who had not moved for hours. She did not doubt that they were standing guard, ensuring she could not escape the man who she could now only assume was Caleb's brother.

She wondered why he had never mentioned his twin. One thing she knew for certain was that this brother had not withstood the same abuse that Caleb had been forced to endure—at least judging by their backs.

She swallowed hard thinking once again of the man who held her captive. He was nothing like Caleb. He was vicious and heartless.

"I have to get out of here," she said out loud.

Once again, she scanned the room, looking for anything heavy enough to drop on the heads of the men below. But the sparsely furnished room held only the platform bed, which would never fit through the small opening, and a spindly wooden chair and chamber pot.

She had ruled out trying to negotiate with her guards. Considering who their leader was, she had no wish to test their mettle. Bad men made bad choices, and she was hoping to avoid them altogether.

Marching to the door, she, once again, tested the latch. Still locked.

Grasping tightly to her fragile control, she renewed her pacing.

What was she going to do? Heart pounding, she looked toward the open casement. Then an idea took form in her mind.

Mayhap the bed couldn't fit through, but she could.

Nostrils flared, she crossed the room to the thin straw mattress and yanked off the wool blanket. Then, she pulled off the remains of her tattered cloak and tied the two together into a makeshift rope, by which she planned to hang out the window and drop down onto the men's heads, hopefully disorienting them enough to allow her to sprint away and disappear into the crowd.

After stretching it out, she knew it wasn't long enough to tie to the bed and extend out the window at a low enough height to make it a somewhat safe drop. Chewing her bottom lip, she scanned her barren surroundings again.

"Fine," she said to herself and dropped her rope. Then, she reached behind her back and started to tug at her laces.

"Damnation!"

She pulled and yanked, bending over, straining to the left, then the right; until she was breathless from her struggles.

"Blast," she cursed again.

It was hopeless. She would never be able to remove her surcote herself, which meant she wouldn't be able to lengthen her rope. Subsequently, there was no way to somewhat safely drop onto the guards' heads, before sprinting into the crowd.

"In naught but my kirtle," she said out loud, shaking her head at her own desperation.

With a sigh, she leaned against the wall and slid to the ground, resting her head in her hands.

Racing nearly naked into a gathering of people was certainly not what Murray or Fritha had in mind when they made her promise not to be reckless. Still, no one had counted on the fact that she was going to be attacked by her enemy, then kidnapped by Caleb's gorgeous but wicked lookalike.

She could hear Fritha tsking at her...*If only ye'd been sensible enough to listen to Caleb and not wander the streets without proper protection.*

Tempest squeezed her eyes shut, trying to silence her racing thoughts. She did not need her conscience to scold her in Fritha's voice. Hindsight had already showed her that leaving The Crescent Moon with Mary and Henry had been a reckless mistake, the price for which she now paid with her freedom. And if she didn't find a way to escape sooner than later, the cost of her error could be greater still—her virtue or even her very life.

Sighing, she dropped her hands listlessly on her lap.

When was she going to learn to be more sensible?

She felt hot and confined, and not just because of the locked door. Tugging at the tight bodice of her surcote left her wanting to screech with frustration.

How was it sensible to be imprisoned in one's own clothing?

She began pacing the room, as Fritha's scolding continued in her mind.

"I'm going to go mad if I don't get out of here!" she cried.

Jerking around, she lunged at the door and pulled back her fist, ready to bang on the slatted wood until she bled. But then she heard a soft knock, and someone whispered, "Tempest."

Recognizing Mary's voice, Tempest's breath hitched. "Aye, I'm here. I'm here!" she whispered excitedly.

A sound so beautiful to rival even a heavenly choir of angels met Tempest's ears—the click of a lock. Heart pounding, she backed away as the door opened and into the room burst Mary and Henry.

Tempest threw her arms around Mary's neck. "I've never been so happy to see anyone in my whole life," she said, beaming. Then she pulled away and mussed Henry's hair affectionately. He blushed in response. An instant later, her smile vanished. She squared her shoulders. "Come," she said, pulling Mary out the door. "Ye can tell me how ye found me later. We must go before—"

"Nay, we mustn't," Mary said in a rush, pulling her back inside.

Henry quietly shut the door. Then he locked it again.

"Ye don't understand," Tempest began, "we cannot delay. Caleb has a brother. He—"

"The Wolf," Mary said knowingly.

Tempest could not have been more surprised. "Ye know about the Wolf?"

Mary nodded. "We have scoured the port looking for ye, checking every tavern and brothel along the way, learning more and more about the enemy as we went along. His real name is Cowen Grant. He's a bounty hunter, a sword for hire, and a rather infamous prize fighter."

"A prize fighter," Tempest exclaimed. "That explains how he was able to best so many men." She seized her friend's hands. "Please," she beseeched. "We must find a way to escape. We must find Caleb. He—"

"He's all right," Mary said, interrupting in a soothing voice. "He came to the tavern believing ye were still locked in my room. Declan and yer men were waiting for him."

Tempest expelled a long breath. Knowing that Caleb was in good company gave her some relief. "Where are they now?"

"Caleb was called out to a duel by a MacKintosh warrior."

"A duel!" Tempest's heart renewed its pounding. She looked at Henry who stood in front of the door.

Mary nodded fervently as she continued, "Caleb thought it best to meet him, believing he might know where to find ye. I tried to tell them that there was a better way, but ye ken how men are. They dismissed my advice and barreled out of the tavern. That was when Henry and I set out to find ye, and here we are."

Tempest struggled to remain calm. "I am grateful to ye, but why are we still here? Why do we not find them?"

Henry stepped forward. "There's no way out, my lady. The Wolf has men in the common room downstairs, out front, and beneath yer casement as I'm sure ye must know."

Brows drawn, Tempest asked, "How were ye able to get the key?"

Mary took a small vial out of her satchel. "'Tis a sleeping draught," she said, smiling mischievously. "'Tis how us lassies take a night off when we need one."

Henry chortled. "Mary walked by the guard outside yer door and smiled. He followed her into an empty room down the hall. 'Tis where he is right now."

"He'll sleep for hours," Mary said knowingly.

"But how will we make our escape?" Tempest asked.

Mary lifted her shoulders. "Honestly, I'm not sure if escape is possible."

Tempest reached for her makeshift rope and showed her companions. "I have a plan. It's terrible, I ken, but at least it's something. I'm going to use this to hang out the casement, then drop on the guards, hopefully rendering them unconscious. I was going to do it earlier, but I couldn't make the rope long enough. But now that ye're here, ye can untie my laces and—"

"Look what I have," Henry said, interrupting with a proud smile while he produced a length of actual rope from his sack.

"Henry, ye're my hero," Tempest exclaimed, reaching for the rope, but Mary quickly grabbed it out of Henry's hand. "Forgive me, my lady, but a good plan never ends with 'hopefully we render them unconscious.'"

Tempest set her hands on her hips. "Then what are we supposed to do? Just wait here until the Wolf returns."

A slow smile spread across Henry's face. "Aye, that's what we should do." He held up the rope. "Because I know how to catch a wolf."

Henry quickly went over the particulars of his plan. It wasn't perfect, but it also wasn't guaranteed to fail—nor did it require Tempest to sprint mostly naked through a crowd of people.

"Let's do it," Tempest said with conviction to her brave companions. Following Henry's instructions, they set to work. Tempest did so with a grateful heart. Never would she have dreamed that her greatest allies, in the greatest fight of her life would be a prostitute and a kitchen lad from Inverness.

Chapter Seventeen

Caleb could no longer hear the horses stomping at the ground nor the snapping of twigs and rustling of leaves. The wind blew but made no sound in his ears. Nothing could overpower the one noise that drowned out all others—the sound of his own heart beating.

For a moment, a flash of his only childhood memory passed fleetingly through his mind. He was laughing and chasing after who he had always believed had been himself. But now he knew he had been playing with his twin brother.

Caleb's chest tightened as he locked eyes with a set so like his own. His whole body stiffened. His breaths remained shallow. Even his lungs were unwilling to open to this new truth that his own eyes could scarce believe.

The man, known as the Wolf, stood in front of Caleb, eying him with hostile confusion. Caleb's mind raced with questions, but he couldn't speak. He could only stare.

It was Laird Munro who broke the silence.

"Excuse me," the older man said, drawing closer, his gaze fixed on the Wolf. "Have you a mark on your forearm, a mark of your birth?"

The absurdity of Laird Munro's question jarred Caleb from his daze. "Now is not the time for yer madness!"

"This cannot wait," The Munro replied as he stepped even closer, standing directly to the side of the Wolf. "Have you a mark of your birth on your arm?" he repeated, his voice soft but intense.

Slowly, the Wolf turned his head, tearing his gaze from Caleb's. "Who wants to know?"

The older man dipped his head in greeting. "I am Laird Donald Munro, and these are my men who have you surrounded."

The Wolf shrugged coolly, despite being so outnumbered. His gaze shifted back to Caleb, but to Caleb's surprise, he pulled on the sleeve of his tunic. Circling his forearm was a shapeless band of deep rose, visible beneath his black, wiry arm hair.

Gasping, Laird Munro pressed a hand to his mouth. "'Tis you," he said, his voice barely above a whisper. His gaze darted between Caleb and the Wolf. "I've searched for you both for so long." Tears flooded his eyes. "You're my children."

Caleb cast Laird Munro a wary glance, but it was the Wolf who spoke first.

"What's this?"

Laird Munro reached out and clamped a hand on the Wolf's shoulder. Caleb's twin jerked away. But Laird Munro persisted. "Your name is Connor," he said to the Wolf. "You are my son." Then he looked at Caleb. "Both of you are my sons."

"Enough madness, old man," Caleb blurted.

"I am not mad," the laird replied, his tone jubilant. "I am your father!"

The Wolf grunted, his gaze scrutinizing Laird Munro's long, lean frame with disdain. "I have a father, old man, and ye're not him."

Laird Munro's face became grave with concern. "You must listen to me, Connor. Whoever this man is, he has deceived you."

"Enough," Alan snarled, coming forward, his sword held at the ready. "I came here for blood!"

"I'm ready to spill some," the Wolf growled, reaching behind his back, and unsheathing his sword. But then the Munro's fist shot up. An instant later, more Munro warriors poured from the wood.

"How many more do ye have hiding?" Declan asked, his wide eyes scanning the glade.

"As many as I need," came the Munro's confident reply.

Caleb, too, scanned the glade. There were now five Munro warriors to every other clan present. It made no difference whether Brodie, MacKintosh, or loyal to the Wolf, they were all vastly outnumbered.

Laird Munro turned his attention to the MacKintosh warrior. "You must be on your way."

"I want vengeance," Alan growled as he glared at the Wolf.

"You shall be joining your laird in the hereafter if you do not heed my words," the Munro said, his voice deadly soft. "And so shall the rest of your men. I will not warn you again."

Alan's face twisted with fury. "This is not over," he said to the Wolf. His hateful glare rested on Caleb, then passed to Declan. At length, he mounted his horse and left the glade. Behind him, his men followed.

Caleb turned back, and once again locked eyes with his brother.

"So ye're Caleb," the Wolf said. His face was impassive, but there was a baiting glean in his eyes. "The spitfire in my room told me about ye, at least in a manner of speaking. Not too long ago, she was kissing me, and apparently, she thought I was ye."

"Tempest," Caleb growled, raising his sword. "Where is she?" Fury pulsed through him as never before.

"Tell us where she is, ye blackguard," Declan demanded as he and Nachlan closed in, flanking Caleb's sides.

"There will be no blood spilled this day!" Laird Munro shouted, coming to stand in between Caleb and the Wolf.

"Where is she?" Caleb hissed, ignoring the man who claimed to be his father.

The Wolf shrugged but gave no answer.

"Brother or not, I will kill ye," Caleb snarled.

"If I'm dead, how will ye find her?" the Wolf asked coolly.

"Please," Declan began in a calmer voice, "she is dear to yer brother."

A slight sneer twisted the Wolf's features as he once more met Caleb's gaze. "I don't care who ye are. I've never given anything away for free."

"We will pay any price," Declan blurted.

The Wolf shrugged. "I'll think on it." He held Caleb's gaze.

Caleb could feel his brother's venom, as if he believed that somehow Caleb had, indeed, stolen his own likeness.

A moment later, the Wolf turned on his heel and motioned to his men.

"Come back here," Caleb snarled.

"Nay, my son," Laird Munro said quietly, coming to stand at Caleb's side.

The Wolf did not stop but carried on walking into the woods.

"We can't let him go," Caleb hissed. "Not now. We've angered him. Tempest will be in even greater danger."

Laird Munro shook his head. "He will not harm her. She's too valuable. He witnessed how well cared for she is and knows we will pay anything for her return."

Caleb did not see Laird Munro give a signal. Still, his men circled close, gathering around Clan Brodie.

Caleb's heart pounded with fury. "Tell yer men to stand down," he snapped at the older man. "I will not let him get away!"

"Now is not the time," Laird Munro said, his voice calm.

Caleb shook his head. "We have her captor here, now. He is outnumbered. He will have no choice but to surrender."

"He would rather die," Laird Munro snapped. "Do you not see that? A man like that does not surrender, and I will not risk the lives of my sons in battle." Laird Munro's voice became more measured as he continued. "My men will find her."

Caleb raked a hand through his hair. "What happens after yer men find her? I cannot see how we will avoid a fight. Ye said so yerself—the Wolf does not surrender."

"His name is Connor and your name—"

"Stop," Caleb snapped. "I'm not yer son. 'Tis impossible."

Laird Munro cocked a brow at Caleb. "Just this morning ye might have said the same about having a twin brother but that has proven to be true."

"This morning ye told me that yer children died."

"I told you my wife died but that my children had been lost to me. The bandits took you."

Caleb's jaw clenched as he fought for control. "How can I suddenly believe this? How can ye? Ye sat across from me this very day, scrutinizing me. I heard no declarations of being yer son then. If I were, indeed, yer child, do ye not think ye would have realized it sooner?"

"You and your brother were only four years of age when you were taken," he explained, his voice calm. "There is nothing in your expression that resembles your mother, but you do have her coloring. And you're the right age. Still, I dismissed the possibility when I cut your bindings earlier and saw no marking around your wrist." His voice grew more intense. "But now...now, I have never been more certain of any truth. You are my sons. Don't you see? Only one of my son's had the identifying mark, and he has it."

Caleb's chest tightened as he witnessed a yearning enter the older man's gaze.

"All these years," Laird Munro continued, "everyone has believed ye and Connor were dead, except for me." His voice and face softened. "I've never given up." He stepped forward. "Please remember me. Remember how well you were once loved."

The fact that Caleb had once been loved was the only thing he had ever remembered before the dark years of his youth.

Laird Munro reached out his hand. Instinctively, Caleb took a step back, dismissing the yearning in his own heart. "We are wasting time," he snapped.

The Munro's hand dropped to his side. He cleared his throat. "I can see your doubt, for which I do not blame you. We shall discuss the matter of your parentage after we have safely retrieved your lady." Laird Munro once again signaled to his men. "More than that, we must see if we can subdue your brother." The Munro turned on his heel and mounted his horse. "We will find her," he promised Caleb before heading toward the forest's edge. His warriors responded straightaway, moving almost in unison as they, too, left the glade.

Caleb watched them go, his heart pounding and his mind racing.

"Are ye alright?" Declan asked, coming to stand at Caleb's side. The older man wore an expression of complete bewilderment.

Caleb breathed out in a rush. His head ached from the speed at which his thoughts raced, but he clung to his focus. "Let us not dwell on what has occurred here in this glade. We have a singular mission—saving Lady Tempest. And brother or not, I will fight him if I must."

Declan's expression shifted to that of concern. "Ye ken he bested half a dozen men."

"I will die for her," Caleb said, his voice unwavering.

Declan reached out and clamped his hand on Caleb's shoulder. "Better that ye both shall live. All men can be reasoned with if one knows what they care about. If we can learn what matters to yer brother, then we will have something with which to bargain for our lady's return."

Caleb shook his head. "Given all we know of him, I'm not certain he has a heart. How are we meant to understand the inner workings of what may not exist?"

Declan's brow furrowed with determination. "We go to the source. Come," he said, before signaling to the Brodie warriors. "Let us catch up to yer father."

"Ye mean, Laird Munro," Caleb said quickly.

"Precisely," Declan replied. Then a smile curved his lips. "Ye ken that if he is yer father that would make ye the son of a laird."

Caleb shook his head, dismissing Declan. "Keep yer mind on our lady." He mounted his horse and followed Declan from the glade. His mind was spinning with countless thoughts and images, his brother's smiling face racing ahead of him as a child, and then the face of his brother scowling at him with naked malice. The declaration of Laird Munro. Lady Tempest—her scorching gaze and full lips. The warmth of her embrace.

Dear God above, but he needed her. And whether he was the son of a laird or a commoner, he was going to find her and never again would he let her go.

Chapter Eighteen

Tempest sat at the open casement keeping watch for the Wolf's return. Her gaze followed the figures below, the guards standing watch, and the many revelers and sailors passing through the street. She pressed her hand to her heart when she spied a young lad with no more than eight or nine years. His face was gaunt, and his limbs as spindly as tree branches. She feared a strong breeze would gather him up and whisk him out to sea. He wore naught but a torn tunic, which hung in tatters just above his boney knees. Even from the story above, she could see the layers of grime covering his face. While people around him were celebrating the holy day with excess, he was clearly searching for a meager bite to sustain his life one more day.

He was not the first beggar child that she had seen while watching for the Wolf to return. Bearing witness to the struggles of the poor and the women like Mary on the street had made Tempest realize the hollowness of many of her own so-called problems.

How often had she complained to Fritha that the surcote she was forced to wear was a prison, or of the countless times she had not listened to the warnings of others who had only meant to safeguard her? Her sheltered existence could never have prepared her for life in the Inverness docks. Now that she truly understood how fortunate she was, she was determined to do more to help others.

She took a deep breath and sat straighter, emboldened by the greater purpose she felt in her heart. No longer did she aspire to be stablemaster. She would certainly always help Arthur and Jacob for the joy of the work. But if she ever returned to Castle Bron, she would dedicate herself to becoming a truly great lady—one who put her people first. More than that, she would do whatever she could to feed the children of Scotland.

Her thoughts turned then to Clan MacKintosh and what a difficult time they had ahead of them. When she and Caleb made it through their present struggle, she planned to send supplies to their neighbor with the hope of mending the rift between their clans.

She looked back in the room where Mary and Henry sat together near the door, ready to launch into action at Tempest's command. The world was so much harder than she ever realized, and yet people were kinder and more courageous than she ever might have guessed. She had only known her new friends for a short while, and yet here they were putting their own lives at risk to save hers. "I owe ye both a great deal."

Mary smiled warmly. "'Tis not every day I get to play the part of the hero and rescue the lady from the terrible wolf. Speaking of wolves, any signs of the one we're hoping to catch?"

Tempest turned back to the street, scanning the ground below for black, wavy hair and broad shoulders. "Nay. Nothing yet." But then she sat straight. "Wait! Aye, 'tis him! He's coming!"

Tempest moved back slightly from the casement ledge to avoid being seen. Her heart quickened as she watched the scene below. Her gaze raked over his strong, lean physique, which was on full display in his black tunic and fitted black hose. The Wolf was so like Caleb. Their features were identical in every respect; however, Tempest suspected that Caleb had never scowled so fiercely.

Tempest glanced back at Mary. "He appears to be in a particularly foul mood." Then her gaze shifted to Henry. "I hope yer trap works as planned, because I don't think he will show us any mercy."

"Do not fash yerself, my lady," Henry assured her.

In that moment, Tempest was struck by the youthful glow of his cheeks. Despite his bravery, he really was just a child. How could she allow a child to stand and fight for her? "Nay," she exclaimed and stood up, her heart pounding. "'Tis folly. Ye both should go, now! Right now! Too much can go wrong." She started to pace. "What happens if we fail? And should we succeed, what do we do once we've trapped him?"

"We'll put a blade to his neck," Mary hissed. "Ye must calm down, my lady."

Tempest shook her head. "Nay, 'tis too reckless. I promised everyone I would think things through, and now I see how flimsy our plan truly is. All he will need to do is call for his men and we will be overrun."

Tempest heard shouting coming from outside. "Blast!" she hissed, her heart pounding harder than ever. Wiping her sweaty palms on her skirts, she knelt and peered out the casement. "Please," she pleaded again while she kept her gaze fixed on the Wolf. "He's unlikely to hurt me, at least not too much, because he can ransom me. But I dare say he'll not spare either of ye."

"We're not leaving without ye." Mary crossed her arms over her chest. "Don't bother insisting. I'm just as stubborn as ye. Anyway, I've dealt with some nasty men in my days. I'm not afraid."

Henry threw his shoulders back and puffed up his narrow chest. "Not me neither!"

Tempest shook her head. "If only we had more time. We should test our plan. We need more time!"

"It will work," Henry assured her.

Tempest took a deep breath. She knew neither Mary nor Henry would back down. They hadn't time to think of another course of action. All they could do was give their current plan all they had. She steeled her shoulders and looked her friends hard in the eyes. "Get in position then and be ready for when he walks through that door."

Tempest could hear nothing over the sound of her pounding heart as she watched the Wolf giving orders. But then one of his men jogged over to him. They stood speaking for several moments before the Wolf followed him down the road and out of sight.

Eyes wide, she glanced back at Mary and Henry. "Angels have answered my prayers. He left!"

"He's gone?" Mary asked. "Are ye certain?"

Tempest nodded. "Quick, let's test the rope again. I'm sure he's not gone far."

Henry sped through the motions of setting off their trap, but the rope stuck.

His breath hitched. He locked eyes with Tempest. "The knot was too tight. Ye were right, my lady."

"Thanks be to Mary and all the Saints," Mary gasped, making the sign of the cross.

After retying the knot, Henry tried again. This time it went off without a hitch. Expelling a rush of air, the lad slid to the ground, resting his back against the wall.

Mary joined him. "When I thought he was on his way, I swear my heart was going to pound straight out of my chest."

Tempest nodded. "Mine, too."

Then a growling sound intruded upon their conversation. Smiling, she cocked a brow at Henry. "It would seem as if ye've already caught a wolf."

Henry blushed. "I'm hungry."

"That reminds me," Mary said as she began fishing around in her satchel. "Here it is," she said, producing a parcel, which she unwrapped, revealing several strips of dried meat.

Tempest eagerly accepted a piece. "I did not realize how hungry I was until this moment." She rested her back against the wall. Swallowing her first bite, she met Mary's gaze. "When all of this is over, will both of ye come home with me to Castle Bron?"

Her face beaming, Mary grabbed Henry's arm. "Truly? To a castle...to yer home?" Mary looked at Henry whose mouth had fallen open. "I do not ken what to say...I...I mean we..." But then she took a deep breath and released her hold on Henry. "Let us not get ahead of ourselves. First, we must carry out an impossible plan and escape the clutches of a notorious prize-fighter."

Tempest cocked a brow at her friend. "My heart is pounding hard enough as it is without yer colorful descriptions."

As if conjured by Mary's words, the shouting renewed outside. Tempest peered out the casement.

The Wolf had returned. "He's back," she hissed, watching while he barked orders at his men. One of them showed him what looked like a ledger of sorts, and he knocked it out of the man's hand and shoved him. Two others grabbed the Wolf's arms, holding him back from presumably pummeling the scribe nigh to death. "And he appears to be angrier than ever." She swallowed hard against the fear building in her mind. He was so strong and tall. How could their plan succeed?

"He's coming closer," she squealed, her heart pounding. "I think he's going to come inside."

He stood in front of the door, but before he stepped from view, he looked up.

They locked eyes.

She gasped.

His cruel gaze burned through her. When he passed from sight, she turned and looked at her friends. "Dear God above, he is coming!"

"Positions then," Mary blurted.

Both she and Henry stood with their backs against the wall, gripping the end of the length of rope. Meanwhile, Tempest stood facing the doorway, her hands on her hips, her stance strong, despite how her legs shook.

Heavy footfalls thundered down the hallway. "Where's her guard?" a deep voice shouted, sending a chill up Tempest's spine. She winced imagining the Wolf's anger when his man finally awoke from his forced slumber. But her pity for the guard was quickly forgotten as the footfalls came to a halt outside her door. Heart pounding, she fought to conceal her fear, forbidding herself from trembling.

The lock clicked. The door swung wide. His black tunic and hose hugged his muscular body, powerful yet sleek. Despite her fear, she held her stance, meeting the Wolf's hard gaze. A dangerous smile curved his lips as he stepped forward, planting his foot unknowingly in the middle of the rope circle on the floor. An instant later, Henry and Mary jerked on the rope. It tightened around his ankle. Then they jumped at the same time, grabbing high up on the other end of the rope, which was suspended over one of the crossbeams, and yanked with all their might. The Wolf's gaze flashed wide the instant before he fell onto his side. Tempest lunged forward, grasping hold of the rope, and together with Henry and Mary, they pulled the Wolf off the ground. When he was dangling upside down, Henry secured the line by wrapping it around one of the sconces on the wall.

"We've got him," the lad yelled.

"Hush," Mary chided.

"Tempest," the Wolf said, his voice strained.

"Ha," she said triumphantly before she grasped the hilt of the Wolf's sword and pulled down, freeing it from the sheath strapped to his back. She circled around her captured prey, feeling every part the proud predator. "I didn't think ye even knew my name." But then Tempest gasped. The Wolf's shirt had fallen, revealing a back covered in scars.

"Caleb!" she cried and dropped to her knees, bringing her face close to his upside-down gaze.

"I've come to rescue ye," Caleb said with a playful smile.

"Ye're off to a great start," she grinned, setting his sword down. "Truly though, 'twas a brilliant plan to pose as yer brother."

"'Twas Declan's idea. Now, would ye mind letting me down?"

"Of course," she said in a rush.

"Wait," Henry said suspiciously. "How can ye be sure he's Caleb and not the Wolf?"

"His back. The scars. Now, quickly, untie..." But then her words trailed off. In that moment, she realized she had him just where she had always wanted him—hanging upside down, completely at her mercy. "Wait, Henry! Don't untie him."

Caleb's eyes shot wide with alarm. "What did ye say?"

She stood back and set her hands at her hips. "Caleb, now that ye can't just walk away from me, I'm going to say my piece. I—"

"Tempest," he began, interrupting.

She dropped to her knees and clamped her hand over his mouth. "Do not interrupt. I will gag ye if need be." Satisfied that he would heed her warning, she let her hand fall into her lap. "I love ye with all my heart—"

"Tempest," he began, his tone more insistent.

"Wheest," she snapped. Then she looked at Henry. "Gag him."

"Nay, lad," Caleb said quickly. "That won't be necessary. I won't interrupt again."

Tempest nodded her approval and lovingly cupped Caleb's upside down cheek. "As I was saying...I love ye. All of ye. And I think ye just don't appreciate how wonderful ye truly are. If ye could only see what I see, ye would know that ye were enough for any lady...for a queen even. Ye're worthy of my love, Caleb, and I only pray I can be worthy of ye. I want ye to be my husband, and before ye deny me again, let me—"

"I accept," he said simply.

"I don't want to hear yer refusals. I..." She faltered, the meaning of his words suddenly ringing clearly in her mind. "What did ye say?"

Warmth flooded his gaze. "I could sooner snuff out every star in the sky than douse the flame burning in my heart for ye. I love ye, and if we can convince Nathan and Elora to permit our marriage...well, then I won't have to steal ye away. Because I will if I have to. I will do whatever I must to call ye my wife."

"Caleb," she squealed and pressed her lips to his—upsidedown, right-side up, their love was true from any angle.

"I'm offended," a harsh voice snapped.

Tempest froze.

She straightened and looked up. Her breath hitched. The Wolf was standing in the doorway.

"Cut me down!" Caleb urged her, but the Wolf shook his head in warning as he walked toward her. "Earlier today, ye said it was me that ye loved." He shrugged his shoulders. "I'm hardly surprised," he continued, his voice cold, "Ladies can be so fickle."

A childish growl rent the air as Henry charged at the Wolf, barreling into him. But his slighter build was no match for the grown man. The Wolf threw the lad to the ground.

"Stop it," Tempest cried. "He's barely more than a child!"

She picked up Caleb's sword and stepped in front of her love, shielding him from his twin.

The Wolf's scowl deepened. "Then the lad shouldn't be playing a man's game." The Wolf's gaze did not waiver. "And neither should ye. Get out of my way!"

"Damn it, cut me down!" Caleb demanded again.

Tempest stood her ground.

The Wolf's eyes narrowed on her. "What is yer name?"

As she gripped Caleb's sword, it occurred to her that challenging a prizefighter to a sword fight might have been the most reckless thing she had ever done. Truly, when was she going to learn to be more prudent?

"My name is Lady Temperance Brodie."

But then again, was now really the time to turn over a new leaf?

She raised Caleb's sword high. "But I'm known as Tempest."

"For the love of all things decent, Tempest, get behind me," Caleb urged as he strained to reach the rope from which he dangled.

"Ye're hanging upside down. How do ye intend to protect me?"

She readied her stance. The Wolf unsheathed his blade. Caleb pushed her aside just as the Wolf swung his sword and cut the rope. Caleb crashed to the floor. The Wolf grabbed her arm and wrenched the blade from her grip with his other hand.

"Release her," Caleb shouted, jumping to his feet.

"Seize him," the Wolf growled. "And the others."

An instant later, the Wolf's men piled into the room.

"Caleb," Tempest cried as three men subdued her betrothed.

The Wolf pinned her arms behind her back. Fighting with all her fury, she strained to free her arms.

"Enough," the Wolf hissed in her ear. "I'm not as kind as my brother."

"Nor am I," she snapped back, continuing her struggle.

"Think of the whore and the child," the Wolf said, his tone deadly soft.

Tempest froze, suddenly aware of Mary's cries. She scanned the room. One of the guards had tossed her over his shoulder.

A string of words that would have made even Tempest blush on another day was spewing from her friend's lips as the warrior carried her out the door. Scanning the room, she looked for Caleb and Henry, but they had already been taken away.

She was alone, once again, with the Wolf. His hold on her went lax. She stepped free from his arms and turned to face him, shoving her finger in his face. "Yer brother officially became my betrothed moments before ye interrupted what was shaping up to be the happiest moment of my life. I have fought too hard to make him mine only to surrender to someone who has the audacity to steal his face. I demand ye release us."

His expression remained cold. "Ye have an army of three, all of whom have been subdued by my men. Ye're not in a position to make demands. And like I told my brother already—I do not give anything away for free."

"Fine," she said, crossing her arms over her chest. "If it is wealth that ye love, more than decency and even kin, then wealth is what ye shall have. Name yer price for our freedom."

"I do not negotiate with women. Now, walk," he said, taking hold of her arm. "Or would ye rather I carry ye over my shoulder?"

Her jaw tensed. Fury raged inside her, but she swallowed the storm. Her temper would be unleashed upon this man, but now, alone and unarmed, was not the time. Gritting her teeth, she stepped from the room and stomped her displeasure down the stairs—all the while, the Wolf held her arm in his vice-like grip.

"Ye're going to have to start negotiating with women because when my sister finds out about this, she is going to be so angry."

"Yer sister?" he scoffed. "Should ye not threaten me with the wrath of yer laird?"

She cocked her brow at him. "Ye've never met my sister. Anyway, Clan Brodie prides itself on its strong ladies."

He shrugged. "I fear no one, man or woman." His tone wasn't arrogant or malicious–it was matter of fact.

She glanced up at him and met his gaze, which was so like Caleb's and yet so different.

Cowen Grant, The Wolf.

A shiver shot up her spine. She did not doubt that he was ruled by something other than honor—whether it was greed or just plain wickedness she did not know. But she knew beyond a doubt that he should not be underestimated.

He kicked open the front door, and she gasped.

Caleb, unfettered, stood flanked by Declan and Nachlan, all with swords raised at the ready, and behind them were the rest of the Brodie guard, along with dozens of other warriors from another clan, all ready to defend her.

Her heart leapt as the sight, but then she cried out as the Wolf pulled her tight against his chest and pricked her neck with the tip of his blade.

"My army has grown," she strained to say.

"Brave words when I could kill ye with a flick of my wrist." He pressed the blade deeper. She swallowed hard and held her tongue.

"Get back," the Wolf hissed.

Declan and Nachlan retreated, joining the other warriors, but Caleb stayed his ground.

She met Caleb's gaze. The power of his love reached across the space between them, filling her heart and fueling her courage, but then his gaze shifted over her head. Fury shaped his features, and she knew he had locked eyes with the Wolf.

"Caleb," she said, drawing his attention back to her. Her gaze bore into his with what she hoped was a message to remain cautious. With Egan dead and Caleb's own demons conquered, his brother was now the only thing keeping Caleb and Tempest apart. But the Wolf was a greater threat than Egan had ever been. She only prayed that Caleb didn't do what she might feel compelled to do if she were in his place—something reckless, like challenging a winning prizefighter to a duel.

Chapter Nineteen

Caleb's fury had never reached such heights as when he saw the brother he never knew put a blade to Tempest's throat.

"Release her," he growled.

The Wolf's face was expressionless while he shook his head.

"Ye're outnumbered," Caleb snapped. "Ye've already lost. Our archers have ye and yer men within their sights. All I need to do is raise my fist."

A slight smile curved the Wolf's lips. "Ye won't give the signal," his brother said, his voice calm.

"Our shared blood will not save ye. Do not test me. I will kill ye!"

"The reason ye won't give the signal has nothing to do with brotherly affection." He tightened his grip on Tempest, making her cry out. "Ye will not risk an arrow marring her flawless skin."

"Listen to me," Caleb began, his heart pounding. "If ye—"

"Nay, brother," the Wolf growled, his mask of control gone. "Ye listen to me. Surrender is never an option, which means I'll have to take my chances and run for it—I may live, or I may die. But she dies, regardless, even if slitting her throat is the last thing I do. So, we have reached a stalemate. I suggest ye come up with another plan."

Caleb clenched his sword tighter. He knew his brother was right. Although the odds were greatly in favor of Clans Brodie and Munro, there was no way to guarantee Tempest's safety if they attacked the Wolf and his men.

Caleb knew what he had to do. "Then it must come down to a single match."

A glint shone in the Wolf's eyes. "Ye will fight me?"

Caleb nodded.

"Nay," Tempest cried but fell silent when the Wolf whispered something in her ear.

"This is madness," Declan said, coming forward.

"Do not interfere," Caleb snapped, flashing Declan a look of warning.

The Wolf smiled. "What happens if I win?"

"Ye and yer men walk away, armed and unharmed," Caleb answered.

"What happens if I lose?" Although there was no trace of arrogance in the Wolf's voice, a hum of laughter arose among his men. Clearly, none believed losing was a possibility.

"Ye and yer men walk away, armed and unharmed," Caleb said, repeating himself. "Either way, win or lose, ye're out of my sight."

His brother's gaze was steady while he seemed to contemplate the terms. Then at length, he said, "I agree but for one exception. If I win, ye come with me. I have a feeling that our father..." The wolf's gaze cut to Laird Munro for a moment, before settling once again on Caleb. "Our true father will want to be reunited with his son."

Caleb shook his head. "I cannot agree to that."

The Wolf shrugged. "Then, we've circled back to where I have a knife to yer true love's throat." He tightened his grip, making Tempest wince.

Caleb's heart pounded in his ears, "Fine," he said quickly. "I agree, but ye must let her go. Now."

"How can I when she is the only thing keeping me alive," the Wolf said calmly.

"Release her to the captain of her guard. I will fight ye. If ye lose, ye walk away. If ye win...I go with ye. Ye have my word." Then Caleb turned addressing his brothers at arms. "Stand down."

After the surrounding warriors lowered their weapons, the Wolf gave Caleb a scrutinizing look. "I have never considered trusting a man's word before, but ye seem foolish enough to believe in fairytales like honor and love." He lowered his blade from Tempest's throat and scanned the warriors. "Which one of ye is the lady's captain?"

Declan came forward. "I am."

The Wolf gave Caleb a hard look. For a moment, Caleb worried that his brother had decided not to trust him after all. But then he shoved Tempest toward Declan who hastened to catch her before she fell.

"Keep back," the Wolf warned. "This is now between my brother and me."

"Caleb, please don't do this. I've seen him fight," Tempest pleaded.

"She's right," Declan began, "I don't believe he wishes ye to go with him. A prizefighter knows no mercy. Every fight is to the death."

Caleb looked back and met Tempest's gaze. "Yer safety is all that matters."

"Nay," she protested. "Yer life matters. Our love matters!"

"Enough," Laird Munro said coming forward. "I'll not stand here and watch my sons kill each other."

Tempest's eyes flashed wide at the older man's words. Then she turned to Caleb and asked. "Who is this man?"

Caleb raked a hand through his hair. "He's...at least, he claims he's my..." He couldn't bring himself to utter the word father as if somehow to speak it would be to make it true, which, at that moment, terrified him almost as much as fighting his brother.

"I'm his father," the Munro said, coming forward. "Laird Donald Munro."

Tempests eyes grew wider still.

"Or rather, I am *their* father," Laird Munro added.

"I grow tired of ye, old man," the Wolf growled. "My father is strong. He's worth ten of ye." Then he turned to Caleb. "We had a deal, or are ye going back on yer word?"

Laird Munro stepped toward the Wolf. "Connor, consider for a moment—"

"That's not my name!"

"'Tis the name I gave ye."

"Ye're not my father," the Wolf growled, raising his sword.

Caleb stepped forward then, shielding Laird Munro. "Tread carefully, brother."

"Fight me so that I can win, and we can leave this place."

"Caleb," Tempest snapped, drawing his gaze. "Where has the good sense that I have long admired in ye gone?"

He raised a brow at her. "My good sense has done nothing but vex ye from the start."

She faltered for a moment before tilting her chin higher. "People can change." Then she set her hands at her hips and squared her shoulders. "I am Lady Temperance Brodie. While ye enjoy the protection of my clan, ye're under my command."

"True," Caleb said. "At least until we are wed and ye vow to honor and obey me."

She froze and looked at him. Despite the precariousness of the moment, he could not help but enjoy the dubious expression on her face.

"On that point, I believe a discussion must be had," she said but then shook her head. "Enough of that for now." She straightened her spine. "I demand ye stand down."

Caleb shook his head. "Nay," he said quietly. "Ye know I cannot do that."

She gave him a hard look. "Are ye truly going to fight yer brother?"

Caleb took a deep breath, and once more locked eyes with the Wolf. Again, his only childhood memory flashed in his mind of what he had once believed was a daydream. But it hadn't been a dream. The face smiling with bright innocence had been his brother, his twin.

Once upon a time, they had laughed together, played together.

Caleb looked at his bride-to-be and felt the truth of her words. Slowly, he sheathed his sword and took a step back. "I yield."

The Wolf's nostrils flared. "What game is this?"

"'Tis not a game," Caleb told him. "Ye've won. I will not fight my brother."

The Wolf lowered his sword and gave Caleb a look of utter disdain. "Such weakness. I will not bring disappointment home to my father." He shook his head in disgust. "I don't need to kill ye. Ye're already dead to me."

In that moment, Caleb realized that he had discovered what mattered most to the Wolf and unknowingly had used it to his own advantage. Whoever the Wolf believed their father to be, clearly, he loved him. More than that, their so-called father was a man who saw weakness where Caleb found strength, explaining why the Wolf had grown into such a hard, self-serving man.

Laird Munro stepped forward. "Connor, listen to me—"

"Enough," the Wolf growled. Then he turned on his heel and stormed toward the line of Munro warriors who stood blocking his way.

"Step aside," Laird Munro ordered. "Let him pass!"

The warriors quickly obeyed, allowing the Wolf and his men to pass through.

Laird Munro called after him. "Connor!"

The Wolf stopped walking but did not look back.

"You are my first born. I smiled down at you with pride while your mother held you and your brother in her arms."

Caleb could hear the hope in the Munro's voice.

The Wolf started walking again.

"You are my son!"

The Wolf turned the corner and disappeared from sight.

The older man sought Caleb's gaze. Caleb's chest tightened as he glimpsed the desperation in Laird Munro's eyes. "After all these years, I finally found him only to lose him again." A look of pleading crossed the man's face. "And what does my other son believe?"

Caleb's mind raced. His heart quickened. He didn't know what to think or say. Then a soft hand slid into his. He looked down at Tempest who was smiling up at him. "Ye were right,

Caleb. Yer memories of being loved were true, and ye're still loved."

Caleb felt his resistance melt. He looked at the man claiming to be his sire, but words of hope remained lodged in his throat.

At length, the Munro said, his voice trembling with feeling. "What say ye?"

Caleb took a deep breath. Fear made him want to look away, but he held fast to his courage and said, his voice barely above a whisper, "Father."

Tears flooded the older man's eyes. He reached out clasping Caleb's shoulder. "Yes, my son."

Caleb's mind raced. His stomach twisted, but he managed to ask the one question he had always wanted to know. "What is my name?"

Laird Munro smiled. "Callum Donald Matthew Munro—but if you prefer, we can still call you Caleb. In this life, it is good to know where you come from but just as important to never forget where you've been."

Fear, joy, love, pain—every emotion Caleb had ever experienced flooded his heart in confusing waves, but it was hope that lingered. Tempest squeezed his hand. His words felt choked in his throat, but after several moments, he met her gaze and said, "I have a name."

She threw her arms around his neck. "Ye have a family!" But then she quickly pulled away and met his gaze. "But ye ken that I have always loved ye. Ye have always been enough for me."

He smiled, "Aye, but if I really am the son of a laird that certainly makes the matter of our marriage simpler."

"There!" Laird Munro said suddenly.

"What?" Caleb and Tempest replied in unison.

Laird Munro beamed as a tear broke past the confines of his lids. "I see her now, in your smile."

"Who do ye see?" Caleb asked.

"Your mother. You have her smile."

Caleb's smile grew.

"I must speak," said one of the Munro warriors, coming forward. He had silver hair, which hung in a thick plait over one shoulder. In his weathered hand, he clasped his sword, the weight of which showed his lean, wiry muscles. "I see her. 'Tis as if our lady is smiling from within ye." The older man knelt on one knee. A breath later he was joined by the rest of the Munro warriors.

Caleb shook his head. "Please, ye needn't...really...I'm just—"

"The son of a laird," Declan boomed, coming forward. His smile was so wide that his eyes crinkled at the sides. "Somehow I am not in the least surprised." Then he, too, knelt, as did every Brodie warrior.

Tempest entwined her fingers with his. "Post the banns," she called out for all to hear. "I'm to be Lady Caleb Callum Donald Matthew Munro."

The warriors from both clans stood and cheered. Caleb scanned the joyful faces, some familiar, some new. Yet all believed, all celebrated. Doubt still nagged at his mind, but he pulled Tempest close and gazed down into her upturned face. The tension eased from his shoulders. With her in his arms, gazing up at him as if he was the sun in her sky, he could believe almost anything. He leaned close and said, "I'm not going to lie. I was looking forward to abducting ye and taking ye away to a small isle, just the two of us."

Her arms wrapped around his neck. "I promise to do something very reckless, and ye'll be forced to take me away for my own good." Her voice dropped lower as she traced a finger along his chin. "Ye might even need to tie me up to keep me from escaping."

A groan fled his lips as he crushed her against his chest. "If ye tempt me like that, then we may not wait until our wedding night."

"Ye promise," she whispered huskily.

"That's it," he blurted as he swept her into his arms. Then he turned to Declan. "I'm abducting Lady Tempest." Next, he met his father's gaze. "I'm familiar with Munro territory, but where is yer keep?"

"Castle Athair is on the coast near—"

"That will do," Caleb said. Then he smiled at Laird Munro. "I'll see ye at home."

"Wait, my lady!" Declan called, after Caleb had started walking away.

He turned back, still holding Tempest in his arms.

"Don't try to stop us," Tempest warned.

The captain of the Brodie guard smiled. "I wouldn't risk yer anger. I only wanted to tell ye to stop by the livery on yer way out of town. Someone is waiting for ye."

"Storm," Tempest exclaimed, smiling.

Caleb smiled back. "I'm quite certain she has missed ye as much as ye have missed her."

"What are ye waiting for then?" Tempest exclaimed. "We've been cooped up in this city far too long. Let's ride!"

~ * ~

They left Inverness and never looked back. His heart flooded with love when they reached the open moors and Tempest spurred Storm to ride faster.

"Everything is how it should be," he said to himself, pushing his horse to catch up. He could feel her joy and it filled him soul-deep.

They rode through the craggy Highlands, over green fields and purple moors until the sun disappeared behind the horizon and myriad shades of pink, lavender, and silver colored the sky.

Within a secluded glen, tucked in a small wood, they made camp for the night. Tempest lovingly wiped Storm down, crooning praise and pressing kisses to the mare's muzzle while Caleb spread out a blanket on the soft earth, upon which he laid dried meat and bannock.

"Not now, Caleb," Tempest rasped, coming up behind him.

He turned and was struck by the beauty of her hair and fair skin in the soft evening light. Pulling her gently into his arms, he said, "I thought ye'd be famished."

Without a word, she stepped from his embrace. A sensual smile upturned one corner of her mouth as she began lifting her tunic. "Mayhap I am."

Seeing her hands shake in the twilight, he reached for her, "My love, we can wait until we have spoken our vows."

She shook her head and stretched her arms high, reaching for the purple sky. "We stand here together, surrounded by greater beauty than could ever be found in a cathedral," she lowered her arms and reached for him as she continued, "with love pure and true in our hearts." She took his hands in hers. "I promise ye, Caleb Munro, here and now, beneath the Heavens that I will love ye and be faithful to ye all the rest of my days."

He had never seen her look more beautiful than in that moment. He cupped her cheek. "I never gave much thought to luck before, but seeing ye standing here, speaking these words to me—I can't help but believe I am the luckiest man alive."

Smiling, she shook her head. "'Tis not luck, which has brought us together. 'Tis destiny."

"Destiny," he breathed. "Ye're my destiny." He stood straighter then and looked deep into her eyes. "Temperance Brodie, I promise ye, here and now, beneath the Heavens that I will love ye and be faithful and never try to dominate ye all the rest of my days."

Her smile widened, and she threw her arms around his neck. "Thank ye for adding that last bit at the end," she whispered, then pulled back a little. He could feel her trembling in his arms. "In words we belong to each other." Then she stepped back and in one fluid motion, she whisked her tunic over her head, revealing her crimson nightdress. "Now, I want ye to make me yers in body."

A groan fled his lips as he crushed her close. Her arms encircled his neck. He seized her mouth in a hungry kiss, penetrating the soft barrier of her lips with his tongue, caressing and tasting in a sensual rhythmic dance that stoked the fires of his desire. He let go of her and pulled away, whisking the nightdress over her head. His breath caught in his throat as his gaze raked over her sloping shoulders, her round, pert breasts, down the curve of her hips to her full, creamy thighs. Nothing could have prepared him for her womanly beauty, so soft, yet so strong.

An alluring glint shone in her eyes as she stepped closer. "Now, 'tis my turn to drink my fill of yer form," she said, her voice husky. She released his belt and lifted his black tunic, then pressed a kiss to his skin. He groaned and jerked his tunic over his head, then pulled off his hose. Her gaze raked over his body with unabashed curiosity and desire, lingering on his hard length.

They came together like thunder, their tongues entwining, their hands exploring, their breaths heaving. Sinking to the ground, their mouths never ceased their kiss. Their arms never stopped holding on as their hunger grew. They were as if one.

One heart.

One love.

When he entered her, they moved in perfect unison, a rhythm as old as time, aching, longing, needing; until they both cried out, lost to the ecstasy of passion that had been burning in their souls for so very long.

Chapter Twenty

Caleb and Tempest rode side by side. Their arms gently extended so that their fingers could weave loosely together. The sun sank low in the sky, casting a silvery haze over the sloping moors. Earlier in the day, they had crossed the River Beauty and ridden past Black Isle. Now, they followed the coast of Cromarty Firth.

Caleb shifted his gaze back to the woman at his side. Tempest's black hair flowed freely down her back. He admired her confident seat as she rocked gently in the saddle in perfect harmony with Storm.

"Castle Athair," Tempest exclaimed when they rounded a jutting point, revealing a long strip of straighter coastline.

Caleb reined in his horse and stared at the distant outline of a castle rising up against the sky, which was painted in dusky hues. Torch fire blazed along the outer wall and atop four towers that rose up from each corner. The stone fortress was as unfamiliar to him as the rest of the surrounding land.

"'Tis grander than Castle Bron," Tempest said with admiration. "Does the sight conjure memories lost?"

Caleb shook his head. "Nay," he began, "I have no memory of this place." His heart started to race. He squeezed her hand tighter. "I'm nervous," he admitted. "What if I'm not welcome, or worse yet, none of this is true. Laird Munro may have been mistaken. I may not truly be his son. I may—"

"Caleb," Tempest said, interrupting. "Give yer fear to the ride."

He gave her a quizzical look. "I don't understand."

Slowly, a smile lit her face until she beamed brighter than any star in the heavens. He could see the fire of her soul in her eyes. "Ye will understand! Just follow me!"

She drove her heals into Storm's flanks and shot ahead. He hesitated for only a moment before urging his own mount to follow. He charged after her. Then he watched her drop her reins, and she flung her arms wide. For a moment, he wanted to push forward so that he could catch up to her and tell her to grab her blasted reins and for pity's sake be more careful.

But he resisted.

"Give yerself to the ride," he said, repeating Tempest's words. "Why not?"

He dropped his own reins and stretched his arms wide. Then he put his head back, raising his face to the silvery sky. Wind whipped at his tunic and coursed briskly over his skin. He breathed deep, and in that moment, he understood.

His fear slipped away. For a moment, he was set free–light, formless, and elusive as the wind.

When they drew close enough to discern the guards at the gatehouse. Tempest slowed Storm to a trot. Pulling his own horse alongside hers, he met her gaze. Her face was flushed, and her eyes shone with vitality.

"Thank ye," he said breathlessly, his heart still pounding from the speed at which they'd raced.

"Are ye ready?" she asked between gulps of air.

He looked at the imposing gate. "Aye," he said simply.

Her smile grew wider still. "Good, because now we cannot delay. Our horses are in need of rest."

He winked. "I see the heart of yer plan now."

Her smile softened. "All jesting aside, are ye ready?"

He shifted his gaze, fixing it on Castle Athair. "I'm coming home."

No sooner had he uttered those words, than the gate began to creak open, and trumpeters appeared at the outer wall. A flourish of fanfare rent the evening. Riding toward them now was a small band of warriors. In front, Caleb recognized his father, Laird Donald Munro.

Donald pulled his horse alongside Caleb's. "Welcome, my son."

Caleb dipped his head in greeting, not trusting himself to speak.

"Come," Donald continued. "We shall ride into the courtyard to greet our people. They await their lost son."

Caleb took a deep breath. He glanced at Tempest. "Go, Caleb Munro!" she said, smiling. "Go to yer people!"

They rode beneath the gate, under the outer wall, and into the courtyard. Caleb's breath caught as scores of people cheered, their faces visible in the surrounding torch fire. The trumpeters continued to play. Munro warriors sounded the motto of their clan. He had no words but watched dumbstruck.

"Smile," Tempest bade him. "Wave to yer people!"

He did as she suggested, and a choir of cheers erupted to new heights of joy. He looked at his father. Tears streamed down the older man's cheeks. Donald reached over and squeezed Caleb's shoulder. "This is a moment I have prayed for but never allowed myself to imagine." Donald's smile widened further still.

Soon, Caleb was being introduced to tacksmen and council members, servants and cottars. He, in turn, introduced Lady Tempest...his betrothed.

Tempest smiled graciously, answered questions, and made thoughtful remarks. Even with her hair unbound and clad as she was in her simple tunic, she was the epitome of poise and ladylike decorum, which coupled with her kind heart, he could not have been more in awe of her. He'd wager even Fritha would have been proud of Tempest at that moment.

"Laird Munro," Tempest said, drawing the laird's attention. She flashed a knowing smile at Caleb before she continued, "Caleb mentioned that ye're betrothed? I look forward to meeting her."

A sad smile curved Donald's lips. He shifted his gaze to meet Caleb's. "Alas, I have broken the betrothal. You see, the lady in question, who I mistakenly believed was in love with you, is in love with your brother. In fact," Donald shifted his gaze to Tempest as he continued, "they had a tryst in the stables, which I believe you may have witnessed, mistaking Connor for Caleb."

Tempest blushed. "Forgive me for asking. I didn't know."

The Munro smiled. "There is nothing to forgive. And with her beauty and the wealth of her family, she will have no trouble finding a more suitable match. Anyway," he continued, his face brightening. "I've decided to hold out for love."

Caleb nodded his approval. "Wise choice, Father."

"What can I say?" the older man chuckled. "I was inspired."

Knowing that his father was speaking of the love he and Tempest shared, Caleb pulled her close in a grateful embrace.

At length, Donald led them to the front stairs of the great hall where Caleb and Tempest followed the laird inside. "There is something I wish to show you," he said to Caleb. "It cannot wait another moment."

Tempest cast Caleb a curious glance. He took her hand, and together they followed Donald. Caleb scanned the great room as they quickly passed through, taking in the numerous trestle tables and tall arched ceilings. Above the grand mantel was the Munro coat of arms. Next, they followed the laird up the steps of the high dais and around the screen into the family rooms. His father seemed to be quickening his pace as if his eagerness to show Caleb whatever he had in mind was increasing with every step.

Finally, they stepped into what appeared to be the solar. Straightaway, Caleb knew why Donald had brought him to that place. Above the fireplace was the portrait of a beautiful dark-haired woman with blue eyes...and a smile Caleb recognized instantly as his own.

Tempest gasped. "'Tis yer mother," she said softly.

A knot formed in Caleb's throat as he approached the painting—tentative at first as if she might disappear into a soft grey fog of dreams. He rested his arm on the mantle and gazed up at her face. Somehow, he could feel her presence. In life he knew that she had loved him as only a mother can love, with her every breath. And still that love surrounded him, for death cannot alter what is so constant and true.

He wasn't certain how long he had stood that way, staring up at his mother when Tempest came up behind him and set her hand on his shoulder.

A soft smile curved her lips. "Laird Munro is going to show me to my chamber." The hint of fire entered her eyes. "It adjoins yers."

"I will see ye shortly," he answered.

She pressed a soft kiss to his lips. Then, she followed his father from the room.

Caleb turned back, and once again, studied the portrait of who he knew without a shadow of doubt was his mother. Then his gaze scanned the other portraits. Surely, they were his grandparents or aunts and uncles. He chuckled out loud, thinking of the crowd of people who had just welcomed him home—him!

He had kin.

He had a name.

For so long, he had believed what he wanted most was to live out his days on a quiet isle, alone. But now he realized that was not truly what he had wanted, only what he thought he deserved. After a lifetime of being told he was worthless, he had never questioned the assertion—that is until a woman as bright and honest as the stars above had told him that she loved him—just as he was.

Suddenly, he had to see her.

He bade his mother goodnight, left the solar, and hastened down the hallway.

"Where is Lady Tempest's chamber," he asked the first servant he encountered.

A maid of no more than ten and five years blushed when she told him, then dipped in a quick curtsy.

"Thank ye," he blurted before bounding down a long hallway and throwing open the last door on the left.

Tempest sat by the fire, running a brush through her hair.

Crossing the room, he took her hand and pulled her to her feet.

"I see the fire in yer eyes," she said, her voice husky.

He pressed her hand to his chest. "I burn for ye." Then he cupped her cheeks and gazed into her beautiful blue eyes. "My past told me I wasn't worthy of ye, and my reason said our love was impossible. But my heart...my heart bade me push through the storm."

She wrapped her arms around his neck. "Now the sky has cleared, and all that remains is what our souls needed most." She pressed a kiss to his lips, then pulled back to gaze into his eyes. "Each other."

"Forever," he whispered and kissed her with all the love in his heart, awakening a storm of passion, which they unleashed upon the other—a thunderous love as mighty as a tempest, as timeless as the stars, and as true as the deepest devotion.

Chapter Twenty One
Epilogue

Tempest reached out her hand, but her fingers did not graze the warm sinews of her husband's masculine chest. She opened her eyes. The bed was empty. Sitting up, she quickly scanned their chamber, but no one else was there. Caleb must have already risen.

A soft smile curled her lips as she laid back and imagined him quietly easing out of bed and taking pains to dress and leave without waking her.

He likely awoke early to ensure preparations were underway for the arrival of their family.

Tempest grinned suddenly as her body came alive with energy. Today, she would see Elora, Nathan, and Cait and meet Cait's new husband, Ewan. With a squeal of delight, she scooted out of bed, crossed the room, and flung open the shutters, letting in the early morning light.

Streaks of gold painted the sky. She took a deep breath and slowly released it again. Then a knock sounded at the door.

"Come in," she called.

"Good morrow, Lady Munro," Fritha said brightly.

"Good morrow, Lady Munro," Mary echoed as she followed Fritha into the room.

"Can ye both stop with the *Lady Munro* nonsense already," Tempest pleaded.

"But 'tis not nonsense," Fritha scolded. "Ye're married."

"Aye," Tempest agreed. "But I'm still me—Tempest will do just fine."

Fritha tilted her head back, casting her gaze to the Heavens as if to appeal to the angels on how best to manage Lady Temperance Munro. But she refrained from scolding and instead crossed to the wardrobe where she withdrew a deep blue tunic.

"Will that compliment my green surcote?" Tempest asked.

Fritha's eyes flashed wide. "Did...did ye just say the word surcote?"

Tempest smiled. "Ye needn't look so shocked."

"Are ye certain ye're well?" Mary asked with a wink to show she was only jesting.

"Very well, indeed," Tempest assured them. "But today is a special day. I wish to honor Clan Munro and my family and dress accordingly."

Tempest had never seen Fritha smile so widely. But as her maid laid the tunic on the bed and walked back to the wardrobe, Tempest's smile faltered. Canting her head, she considered her maid's appearance. Normally, Fritha's hair was pulled back in a severe knot on top of her head, and the constant look of worry made her skin look pale and drawn. But today, Fritha's hair was loosely plaited and coiled at the nape of her neck. Tendrils framed her flushed cheeks. Her eyes seemed brighter, and her movements were smooth and easy.

"Fritha," she said absently while she continued to study her maid. "Ye look different somehow."

Fritha blushed but shrugged off Tempest's comments before turning her attention back to the wardrobe. Meanwhile, Mary caught Tempest's gaze and motioned for Tempest to join her near the casement.

"Gaze with me upon the horizon, my lady. Surely, 'tis the start to a lovely day," Mary said casually, but then she dropped her voice to a whisper. "Fritha is in love!"

Tempest's eyes flashed wide. She glanced back at her maid who was still busy sorting fabrics, then shifted her gaze back to Mary's. "The sky promises a clear day to be sure," she said loudly. Then she, too, whispered. "Tell me everything!"

"I've noticed a certain man's gaze following her about the great hall. And yesterday, he stopped and spoke with her for some time while she was collecting herbs in the gardens near the kitchen."

"Which man?" Tempest quietly urged her, nigh giddy with anticipation.

"Laird Munro," Mary whispered.

"Laird Munro," Tempest blurted aloud.

Fritha whirled about, her expression distressed. "Pardon?" she said.

Tempest cleared her throat. "Er...Laird Munro—I must speak with him about today's menu. Do either of ye know where I might find him?"

Fritha shook her head. "Why would I know the whereabouts of the laird? 'Tis no business of mine. Mayhap ask Henry. That lad follows the laird around like a loyal pup."

Mary cleared her throat. "I believe he and Caleb were standing watch on the ramparts for the arrival of our guests."

Tempest smiled, fighting to contain her excitement over the secret romance between her uptight maid and the clan's laird. "I shall join them as soon as I'm dressed."

Fritha came forward then, cradling a deep green surcote. "For yer hair, it would be lovely to plait it in sections, then pile—"

"Nay," Tempest said, interrupting. "I shall where my hair down as always."

"But ye said ye wished to present yerself more formally—" Fritha began.

Tempest set her hands on her hips. "I will concede to certain conventions for the sake of honoring my clan. I may don a surcote for special occasions and make certain that Storm is saddled before I ride her...most of the time anyway. But there are limits. I'm still me, and Caleb loves me for who I am."

Fritha's face was impassive for a moment. Then a gentle smile curved her lips. She crossed the room and planted a kiss on Tempest's cheek. "So do I. I am so proud of ye...Lady *Tempest*."

Tempest pulled Fritha into a hug. "Thank ye," she said, her heart flooded by Fritha's kind words. Then Tempest stepped back, giving her maid an appraising look. "Yer hair looks lovely like that, all soft and wispy."

Her maid blushed and touched a shaky hand to the loose tendril at her temple. "Thank ye," she said quickly before clearing her throat. "Now then, enough of this nonsense. We must finish, for yer family comes this day!"

Tempest smiled so hard it made her cheeks ache. "I cannot wait to see Elora and Cait!" She turned so that Fritha could tie her laces.

"Finished," her maid said as she stepped back.

Tempest smoothed her hands over her embroidered surcote. "Am I presentable?"

Mary chuckled. "Ye're a vision. Now, go! I can feel yer excitement from across the room."

Fritha chuckled. "Aye," she laughed. "Go before ye erupt and we're caught up in the storm!"

Tempest planted kisses on both their cheeks before she quickly made her way to the ramparts where she found Caleb and Donald standing together, both clad in the Munro plaid.

"Any signs of them," she asked breathlessly, taking her place beside Caleb.

"Not yet," he said, smiling down at her.

She fixed her gaze on the horizon, waiting for the first sign of the Brodie, Campbell, or MacLeod banners. She could hardly wait another moment to see Elora.

"I ken exactly what Elora will say when I see her," Tempest said excitedly.

Caleb smiled. "And what is that?"

"She will say that I look the part of Lady of Castle Athair but will be relieved that I still look like me."

He chuckled. "I dare say ye're right." He cleared his throat. "Now, what will she say to me."

Tempest smiled. "She will hug ye, and call ye brother."

Caleb laughed. "Let us hope ye're right, and what will Nathan say?"

Tempest's laughter mingled with his. "He will claim to have known all along that ye were the son of a laird."

Caleb threw his head back, laughing all the harder.

Donald smiled at them. "I am glad for you both. 'Tis a hardship to be separated from family."

Tempest beamed at her new father-in-law. "Remember, they are yer family now, too. We will all, at last, be together."

Her smile faltered when a shadow passed over Donald's face. She squeezed his hand. "I'm so sorry that we've had no luck finding Connor. Ye mustn't give up hope."

Donald took a deep breath. His face brightened. "Never," he vowed. "I'll never give up hope. One day, my eldest son will stand here on these ramparts, and he will take his rightful place as Laird of Castle Athair."

Caleb smiled. "That day will come, father. I've no doubt." He wrapped his arm around Tempest. Her heart quickened as his gaze met hers. She could see the love for her in his eyes burning as bright as fire.

He cupped her cheek as he continued, "For I know better than most men that love makes anything possible."

Thank you for reading *The Tempest, Rebel Hearts Book Three*. What's next? Keep reading to find out!

The Wolf, Rebel Hearts, Book Four

Coming Soon!
Don't miss the release of The Wolf.
You can follow Lily Baldwin on Bookbub

For your reading enjoyment, meet The Scottish Outlaws.

They are Scotland's secret rebels.

A band of Highland brothers who will never surrender...

Before King Edward of England sacked Jack MacVie's beloved city of Berwick upon Tweed, Jack had lived a quiet life, setting sail each morning to fish the waters of the North Sea, alongside Quinn, one of his four brothers. Muscles straining, heart pounding, he would haul in the day's catch as the sun shone on his brow and salty breezes filled his lungs. Waves would crash against the ship's hull while gulls cried shrilly, mingling with the never-ceasing music of the sea.

How he missed her song.

Long had it been since he had gripped a sodden net or heard fish slapping their breathless bodies upon the deck, for the English king's merciless deeds had driven him toward a new profession.

Now, he was one of Scotland's secret rebels.

Still, his heartstrings could pluck the ocean's rhythmic sounds, which were harbored deep in his memory, never to be forgotten.

But at that moment, he needed to quiet the waves lapping gently in his mind. Now was not the time for memories. He drew a deep breath, becoming aware of the forest sounds surrounding him.

Hooves pounded the earth in the distance.

Now was the time for action.

Jack shook his head. "I miss being a fisherman." Lowering his black hooded mask over his face, he glanced back at his four brothers. Their horses snorted and stomped at the ground. "Saints, masks on," he hissed. "Stick to the code. Ye're called by yer saint's name. We are Scottish rebels, not murders. Remember yerselves, lads." Narrowing his eyes to see through the slits in his mask, Jack scanned the ribbon of road beyond the trees. The English noble's carriage they had been tracking careened into view along with half a dozen guards.

Quinn nosed his horse forward, stopping beside Jack. "The hour grows late. They appear to be in a hurry to reach the next village before dark."

Jack stretched his neck to one side and then the other. He took up his reins. "'Tis a pity we'll have to delay them." Kicking his horse in the flanks, he and his brothers surged forward, but then the second youngest, Rory, shot ahead.

"Damn his reckless hide," Jack snapped. "What the devil is wrong with him?"

"He's going to collide with the carriage," Quinn shouted.

Without slowing his horse, Jack dropped the reins and cupped his hands around his mouth, shouting to Rory through the fabric of his mask, "Pull back, St. Thomas." But either Rory did not hear his warning or chose to ignore it. Bending low in his saddle, Jack urged his horse faster to catch his wayward brother, but it was too late. Jack cursed as Rory shot through the trees into the open road straight into the carriage's path. Rory's horse reared up on its hind legs. A shout went up from the carriage driver while the guards whirled to meet Rory's blade.

Another cry from the driver grabbed Jack's attention. The carriage rocked, then listed hard right. The driver pulled back, but the vehicle bounced to the left, the right wheels airborne for an instant, then it toppled onto its side and skidded.

Jack reached the roadside at a gallop and met the guards head on. Steel rang in a harsh clash. Fury swept through him.

A guard charged at Jack. He parried, then swung. The flat side of his sword slammed his attacker's forearm. The enemy's blade dropped to the ground.

One guard disarmed.

Jack swung around, his sword carving into a shoulder. Another enemy blade dropped.

One guard maimed.

Sword raised high, he readied for the next assault, but only a cloud of dust stirred. He scanned his brothers—none injured, all had kept their seats. Then he eyed the guards on the ground—none dead. With a grunt of approval, Jack swung down from his horse. His brothers followed.

In the fading light of day, Jack knew they were a terrific sight. They were all large men, and Ian, the youngest brother, at only nineteen stood a hand taller than Jack who was already well over six feet in height. They wore black tunics covered in gleaming black mail, black hose, tall black boots, and black hooded masks, and about their necks hung large wooden crosses.

"St. John," Jack said to Ian. "Secure the guard."

"Aye," Ian answered. With rope in hand, he turned on the guards whose eyes bulged at his approach, clearly terrified by Ian's size. Jack couldn't help the smile that curved his lips at the sight. What the guards didn't know was that despite Ian's towering height and breadth of shoulder, he was as gentle as a lamb—unless provoked. Jack's smile faltered. He needed to stay focused to ensure their mission went swiftly and smoothly. He did not want any unnecessary bloodshed.

Turning to his middle brother, Alec, Jack said, "St. Paul, check the carriage. Make certain no one was injured when it overturned."

With a curt nod, Alec crossed to the toppled carriage.

Next, Jack motioned to Rory. "St. Thomas, gather the weapons." And then to Quinn he said, "St. Augustine, take up collection."

A loud screech drew Jack's attention back to the carriage. "St. Paul," he said to Alec. "What the hell is going on?"

A moment later, Alec pulled a thrashing mass of silk and lace from the carriage. He set the lady on her feet. She screamed and lashed out, her fingers bent into claws. Alec seized her arms, pinning them behind her back.

"St. Paul, release her," Jack ordered.

With a shrug, Alec dropped her hands and stepped back. The lady screeched and shifted her gaze to Jack. "St. Paul, St. John—You are no saints. How dare you make a mockery of what is holy?"

Jack turned his back on her. He was certainly not going to give audience to a selfish noblewoman's ideas of devotion.

At his dismissal, she snarled her fury. "I am Lady Eleanor de Clare. You will feel the full wrath of King Edward. You worthless, Scottish—"

Jack turned and lunged forward, bringing his masked face inches from hers. "I have already felt the full wrath of your King, which is why ye're feeling mine." He closed his eyes, reclaiming his control. He would not take his fury out on a woman. Taking a step back, he looked at Quinn who riffled through one of her trunks. "What has she given to our cause?"

"A handsome bag of coin, but that is all," he answered.

Jack turned back to her. He grasped the wimple she wore. She shrank away as he rubbed the fabric between his fingers. No finer silk had he ever felt. He lifted his gaze to her face. Although he guessed she had as many as five and thirty years, her beauty had yet to fade. He met her cold, blue eyes and reached down, seizing her fingers. Three rings with gems the size of blackberries gleamed even in the dim light. She yanked to pull her hand free, but he grabbed her wrist and held her still while he worked the rings from her fingers. He dropped her hand, and it flew to her throat. Jack reached for her.

"Stay back you Scottish bastard!"

He shoved her hand aside. His fingers made contact with a string of pearls lying on skin as smooth as velvet. His gaze dropped from her neck to her chest, raking across her display of rounded flesh, pressing with her every exhale against the bold cut of her bodice. Then he reached behind her neck, slowly grazing her silken skin, and unclasped the string of pearls. "Scotland thanks ye, my lady."

Jack handed the jewels to Quinn. "Add these to the lot."

Ignoring the lady's insults, his gaze scanned the bound guards with approval. It would be some time before she was able to free one of her men. Then, they would still have their wounds to dress and the carriage to right before her ladyship could be on her way.

Crossing the road, he swung up on his horse. "Saints," he called to his brothers. "Let's ride!"

Like swiftly moving black waves, they barreled deep into the forest, leaving the road behind. Before too long, they would be back at their hideaway where they could rest and ready themselves for the next English noble who rode north into Scotland.

But until then, Jack would be free to imagine that he was once more at sea and the city he loved had never been turned to ash.

You can find Jack and the rest of his brothers on Amazon. Wishing you joy and many blessings! All my best, Lily.

More by Lily Baldwin
The Scottish Outlaws:
Jack: A Scottish Outlaw
Quinn: A Scottish Outlaw
Rory: A Scottish Outlaw
Alec: A Scottish Outlaw
Rose: A Scottish Outlaw
Ian: A Scottish Outlaw

~ * ~

Rebel Hearts Series:
The Renegade
The Piper
The Tempest

~ * ~

The Isle of Mull Series:
To Bewitch a Highlander
Highland Thunder
To Love a Warrior

~ * ~

A Jewel in the Vaults
The Devil in Plaid
The Courageous Highlander
Highland Shadows

~ * ~

The Ultimate Historical Romance Lovers Activity Book

Made in United States
Troutdale, OR
07/19/2023

11413635R00137